2222

Ken Kroes

Editor: Irene Kavanagh http://www.editors.ca/profile/7624/irene-kavanagh
Cover Design: SelfPubBookCovers.com/Lori
Book design by Ken Kroes

ISBN: 978-0-9940332-1-5
Publisher 1779671 Alberta Inc.

www.the2222book.com

ACKNOWLEDGMENTS

I would like to personally thank my editor, Irene. Her extreme patience, encouragement and hard work led to an outstanding working relationship and a final product that I am very proud of.

1 - A NEW BEGINNING

Do you ever get that uneasy feeling that someone is watching you, or that some danger is nearby? The feeling that makes the hairs stand up on the back of your neck or a shiver go through your body. These instances are considered paranormal, or fringe studies, by mainstream science, and if you ask your friends, many will acknowledge that they have experienced similar feelings. On the other hand, if you could ask animals in the wild the same question, they would reply, "Of course!" Their intrinsic life skills have been honed over millennia through the process of evolution and survival of the fittest.

A few hours before dawn, a sense of disquiet engulfed the leader of the wolf pack. He lay crouched in the underbrush near a herd of cattle—easy prey—resting on a hillside. After centuries of domestication, their ability to sense lurking danger was diminished, and they were ill-equipped to run or fight off the pack's hunting skills.

His senses did not mislead him. From the guard tower, a few hundred yards away, his head had been placed squarely in the crosshairs of Alec's rifle. Alec and Jordan were nearing the end of their evening shift and had noticed motion in the bush near the resting herd. They used their binoculars to spot a few of the wolves. Then, with practiced skill, Alec coaxed his cold muscles to stop shivering long enough to get one of them in his rifle sights. As his finger tightened on the trigger, the wolf turned and looked directly at him through the scope.

How can he know . . . there's no way he can hear me. Within a split second, Alec lowered the crosshairs a fraction and squeezed the trigger. The shot missed the wolf by several feet, but the blast sound and the nearby eruption of dirt from the bullet's impact startled the pack causing them to make a hasty retreat to the safety of the forest.

"Missed!" Alec said with mocked frustration as he tried to rationalize in his mind what had just happened. Somehow, the wolf knew Alec had him fixed in his sights and by some unknown means, during that moment of eye contact, had convinced Alec to spare his life.

"Need a bit more time at the range?" Jordan quipped,

"Yeah, right. He moved just as I pulled the trigger, but at least they're gone now and won't be back for a while."

After the incident, the rest of their shift passed quietly as they continued to scan for new intruders. Their replacements arrived a few minutes early, and they were relieved to head back to the barracks and warm up.

The sun was just beginning to appear as they approached the defense complex, nicknamed "the DC." It covered some one hundred acres and was surrounded by two tall, galvanized steel fences twenty feet apart, the outer one topped with rolled razor wire. Located a few miles from Epoch, their village, the DC contained defense training areas, barracks, the city jail, horse stables, and a few office buildings.

Entering through the main gate, they passed a drill sergeant taking great pride in making life as miserable as possible for a group of new recruits.

"I sure don't miss that," Alec said, recalling two years earlier when he and Jordan endured boot camp with the same drill sergeant. Alec had never had any interest in joining the DC, but boot camp attendance was mandatory for all sixteen-year-old able-bodied young men. Afterward, they were required to serve in the Reserves and report for a few weeks of duty a couple of times each year. This usually meant defending the nearby farms from predators or poachers from the smaller villages surrounding Epoch.

"Me neither," Jordan replied. "I once thought I'd like to make a career out of this, but boot camp convinced me otherwise. The only way that I'd join full time now is if it was in some type of command position, but you need to serve for years first. I guess I'll just have to be content with being part of the Reserves even though the assignments are boring. I'm glad to be done with this rotation and looking forward to being back home tonight."

"Yeah, home will be good," Alec agreed. "So will sleeping at night and working inside during the day."

They approached the Reserves building where they stayed during their rotation. The building wasn't in the best condition, needing both restoration and paint. A large, new poster had been painted on the outside entrance wall and stood out starkly. The DC commander's image had been painted above a slogan. He appeared to be shouting, "Join Now!" His finger pointed directly outward. The same poster had been painted in several prominent places throughout Epoch to attract more recruits for full-time enrollment. Labor was in short supply, and there was stiff competition with businesses to recruit people to join the DC.

After hot showers, Alec and Jordan ate at the mess hall and slept for a few hours before jumping on a supply wagon heading towards Epoch. They were dropped off at the outskirts of town close to the Re-Discovery Center, where both had their regular jobs. From there, they slung their duffle bags over their shoulders and started down the winding cement walkway through the campus and towards the transit stop.

The spring afternoon was perfect, with the sun still above the hills and a warm breeze meandering over the grass and through the nearby trees. The campus was smaller in size than the DC, with only a dozen or so brick buildings, but it had more history. It had been built when Epoch was first formed and had beautifully manicured lawns with several rose beds, exotic plants, and an abundance of water features. Other than the birds, rippling water, and fluttering leaves, there wasn't another sound to be heard. There were no roaring car engines, honking horns, or droning airplanes, all for the obvious reason—none of these things existed.

A distant yell shattered the idyllic setting. "Hey, Alec!" He saw Allison running towards them followed closely by Kimberly, her best friend. As soon as they had caught up, Kimberly put her arm around Jordan's waist and kissed his cheek. Allison approached Alec as though he were prey, just as a wolf would move towards a herd of cattle. She was beautiful, smart, and made it clear that she liked Alec, who remained elusive about relationships.

“Hi Allison," he said. “How have things been?”

“Not bad, but everything just got so much better!" Her tone was teasing, and she smiled coyly. “It’s been a long few weeks with you gone.”

Alec couldn’t help but smile back, willingly caught in her trap.

“How’d things to at the DC?” Kimberly asked Jordan, as she motioned towards his duffel bag.

“Two weeks of cold night shifts guarding herds of cattle,” he lamented. “The only real excitement was a pack of wolves last night, which our sharpshooter over here somehow completely missed.”

Alec nodded his head slowly. “Fine,” he challenged. “Next rotation, you can have the first shot, and we’ll see how *you* do!"

“We’ll see!” Jordan countered then turned towards Allison. “How are things going here—anything that we need to know?”

“No, just the usual, a big push to get things done faster with fewer people, but no major breakthroughs. It’s Friday, though, and I don’t want to talk about work.” She caught Alec yawning. “Did you two get any sleep after working all night?”

“Not much—sleep is overrated anyway,” Alec replied. “I’ll catch up tonight.” Sensing her disappointment, he added, “But we’re still on for our date tomorrow night, right?”

“Of course! I guess I’ll let you rest tonight, but you better be bright-eyed tomorrow.” She squeezed his hand affectionately.

The four continued down the path to the transit center where a small group of people had already gathered waiting for the next tram. The trams, or street cars, were powered by an underground cable system similar to that used for trolleys in San Francisco before the Great Loss and were the only mechanical transportation system in Epoch.

"My parents are having a barbecue next weekend," Allison said, "Would you both like to come over?"

Kimberly tugged Jordan's arm lightly, and her glance signaled the expectation that he would be there. Alec picked up the wordless cue and decided to go along with what he knew was a setup.

"Sure, sounds like fun," he replied disingenuously. "Maybe we could do a little jamming as well." He enjoyed playing piano and guitar, and his near-perfect pitch made him a popular guest at social gatherings.

Allison beamed. "Absolutely! I don't think we would've had much choice anyway, since your grandma will be there, and she'll insist on entertainment."

The tram rumbled up to the transit stop, and people climbed on and off before it continued its scheduled path. Its route snaked along roads in the residential area of Epoch and then went through the commerce area of the village which bordered Skater Lake. There were no cars in Epoch, but the roads were designed in anticipation of their arrival along with side streets and main thoroughfares to accommodate the planned growth of the community. As the tram passed row upon row of family-sized homes, Allison and Kimberly immersed themselves in the details of the upcoming barbecue, while Alec and Jordan talked about the project they were working on in their spare time.

"You able to work at the shed this weekend?" Alec asked.

"Sunday for sure, but tomorrow I promised your dad I'd help out with stuff around the town hall."

"He tried to talk me into that too, right before we left for our rotation, but I didn't commit to anything," Alec said. "It feels like weeks since we've done anything on the plane, and at this rate I don't know if we'll ever get finished."

Since they first learned about planes in school, their minds had been in the clouds. Though automobiles were anticipated to be built soon, they interest was focused in flying and building Epoch's first airplane. At first, they had thought of constructing a hot airship, but decided that it wouldn't serve their long-range exploring plans. After fixing up an old shed near the lake a couple of years earlier, they had begun to build the basic structure of a two-seater plane that could take off and land on the water. It was a long process and a lot of work, with everything needing to be hand-made including the frame, engine, and controls. Their hopes were to finish within the year to coincide with the research on fuel and engines being done at the Re-Discovery Center.

The tram came to a stop, and the girls stepped off, waving as they stood on the road. "See you tomorrow, Alec," Allison shouted as the tram pulled away.

Jordan watched Alec wave back. "You might as well give in. I don't think you have any choice in having Allison as a girlfriend."

"I guess you're right," Alec said, smiling. "She's persistent—I'll have to give her that."

The tram entered the center of the village which had a collection of privately run shops, a church, the town hall, bank, water tower, and the main entrance to the warehouse. Several armed guards and the usual crowd stood around the entrance, waiting patiently while holding onto their ration slips. After several stops, the tram made a sharp turn and headed along the road that ran beside the lake. It passed a few restaurants and bars already busy with Friday afternoon patrons along with groups of people walking on each side of the road enjoying the spring weather.

Alec was lost in thought as he looked out the back of the tram. The feeling of being watched crept over him, and he turned to look directly at a Labrador Retriever sitting on the curb. The dog wore no collar, and despite plenty of opportunity for distraction, seemed to be attentively looking back at him.

This can't be—surely he's just watching the tram.

As he passed the dog, it became clear that it wasn't the tram the animal was watching, but him specifically. Their eyes stayed locked on one another until the tram turned onto a side street. When the eye contact broke Alec had a brief nervous feeling that the dog was not actually looking at him but was actually looking out *for* him, in a protective manner.

My mind must be playing tricks on me due to lack of sleep.

After a few more streets and turns, and with the lake behind them, Jordan and Alec got off the tram.

"See you Sunday," said Jordan.

"You bet." Alec replied absently. They parted ways to walk to their homes only a few blocks apart. He still felt unsettled. When he had almost reached his house, one of the larger ones in Epoch, he was greeted by Koda, his small but energetic dog.

He stopped to offer the obligatory ear scratches while receiving a good face cleaning from Koda's tongue. Their greeting ritual complete, they climbed the front steps and entered the house where his mother was busy setting the dinner table.

"Hi, Alec," she greeted. "I'm glad you made it home for supper and to take care of that dog of yours. He's been driving me crazy all day—like he knew you were coming back."

Alec thought about what his mother had just said. *The wolf early this morning—then the dog on the road, and now Koda. What's going on?*

"Yeah, hi..." His nose caught the aroma of roast beef and fresh bread, and he let himself forget everything for the moment. He realized how hungry he was and how much he had missed home cooking after being away for two weeks. He washed up hurriedly. When he returned downstairs, his parents and siblings were already at the table. His father, Jake, was eager for news. "Good to have you back, Alec. How did your rotation go? Anything exciting going on?"

"Just another rotation of night shifts guarding cattle and sheep," Alec replied without much enthusiasm.

"Well, you can fill me in tomorrow while we're working at the town hall."

"I think Jordan is helping you tomorrow, Dad. I'm planning on working on the plane."

His father's face showed disappointment. "But there'll be time enough to work on your hobby this winter. I could use help now working out Epoch's wages, prices, and labor to help balance things. It's been almost a year since this was last done, and with things changing so rapidly, we must make sure that things line up well."

Alec sighed, "I haven't worked on the plane for over three weeks, and I honestly don't feel like cranking out numbers all day tomorrow." Before he finished answering, he realized that his tired mind had made a big mistake.

"Don't feel like it?" His father's voice rose in anger. "Alec, you need to grow up and sort out what you're going to make of yourself. You can't expect to tinker around at the Re-Discovery Center and working on hobbies for the rest of your life. You don't even realize or appreciate the opportunities you have. I can arrange for you to have a very good position in town government, maybe even someday have my job."

Alec almost spoke again without thinking. He wanted to tell his father that he had no interest or desire to work in the town's government offices and that working for the rest of his life at the Re-Discovery Center was exactly what he planned on doing. But he didn't have the energy for the argument this would have caused, so he bit his lip. "Ok, Dad, I'll help you and Jordan tomorrow."

Jake wasn't completely satisfied with Alec's tone, but accepted his answer. "That's better. We'll have fun working on this together—you won't regret it." He proceeded to give the mealtime blessing.

While his father prayed, Alec beat himself up for giving in so quickly. In doing so, he surrendered a whole precious day of work on the plane. His darkening mood shifted deeper into other things he was unhappy about—reciting grace for one. *What's the point of saying grace before each meal?* He attended church every week, not that he had a choice, but he questioned the teaching there against what he knew to be fact based on science. Saying grace seemed meaningless.

He wasn't alone in his thoughts. Most of the old families in Epoch were strongly Christian in faith, but with more science and technology appearing, people in Alec's age group were not as entrenched as the older generation in the bible and church teachings. This attitude was growing despite the efforts of church elders to return religious faith to as strong a force as it had been right after the Great Loss.

Alec's thoughts tuned back to the real world just as his father finished the prayer, and copious amounts of food flowed from platters and bowls onto everyone's plates.

Alec's mother, Claire, tried to change both the subject and the mood of the moment. "Allison's mom called me to today and invited us to a barbeque this weekend," she said cheerfully.

"So I heard," Alec said.

"She's such a nice girl. I do like her a lot," his mother commented.

"You should bring her over more often so we can get to know her better." Jake spoke half-jokingly, knowing that Alec had been avoiding Allison's advances.

"Does Alec have a girlfriend?" his youngest brother asked.

"Not yet, dear," Claire replied with a small laugh. Alec ignored all the good-natured bantering and purposefully concentrated on the meal in front of him.

After dinner, the absence of television and computers drove all of them to scramble off in their own directions to find activities. Claire went to her sewing room to work on a dress she was making for Alec's sister. The rest of his siblings went to attend a play being performed in the town hall. Jake followed his regular routine of retiring to his study to review the village reports.

Jake had worked hard for the last fifteen years to reach his position of Epoch Manager. Although not an elected position, he saw it as a powerful one since it was he whom the elected officials turned to for advice and relied on to manage day-to-day affairs. His work included setting prices and wages for the businesses run by the community, controlling staffing levels for schools and the hospital, and prioritizing work at the Re-Discovery Center. He took pride in his job and enjoyed the prestige, power, and wealth that came with it. All factors that had increased as Epoch had grown quickly since he had taken charge.

The people of Epoch knew and understood the difficulties in his job as well as some of the hard decisions he was obliged to make with limited resources, but they didn't know about everything. Jake and previous town managers had made many decisions to ensure the survival and growth of the town that undoubtedly would have appalled people. As he reviewed the latest census numbers and labor reports, he knew he would have to continue with at least one of these secrets for a while, yet surprisingly, it didn't seem to bother him as much as it probably should have.

When he finished working on the labor reports, he came across a memo from the commander of the DC that had been sent to him as well as all the elected officials. He didn't think much about it until he came upon one sentence.

"… Furthermore, to provide adequate protection to both the town of Epoch and its surrounding farms, my recommendation is that we increase the compulsory reserve-service time from two to four months per year and increase our current operating budget by 25% to attract permanent recruits…."

"How dare he!" Jake hollered aloud. "He should've discussed this with me first—and there's no way we're going to increase the DC's budget by that much. Far more important things are needed!"

He wrote a note to himself to set up appointments with the elected officials. They'd need reminding that there had been no military threat of any kind throughout the 200 years since the Great Loss and that the current budget for the DC was probably too high and should be reduced. He also made a mental note to secretly enlist one of his trusted staff to do a bit of graffiti work on the new "Join Now!" posters recently painted on a few downtown buildings.

"That will get him going," he muttered and then dove into the remaining pile of paperwork.

Alec followed his siblings to the town hall but would not be seeing the play. Instead, when they arrived, he detoured to a room in the back of the building where a shortwave radio station had been set up when Epoch was first established. Immediately after the Great Loss, there was a lot of communication with people across the world, but as the years passed, the number had steadily dwindled until now there were less than ten other sites still on the air. There were people in Epoch who continued to scan for new sites and daily set times when known sites came online. The day's affairs were discussed, and help could often be found by sharing as much information as possible. Since Epoch was much larger than most places, more advanced technically, and had access to more resources, its inhabitants usually provided knowledge to others.

Alec had volunteered for many evening shifts in the radio room and looked forward to talking to people he had never met. During this time of year, his shifts lasted through the time that the Smokey Mountains site, and a site in Brazil, were online.

"Hi Alec, how are things up in the northwest today?" asked Brian from the Smoky Mountains.

"Gorgeous spring day up here," Alec said. "Has that fire died down yet?" He had heard about the forest fire that veered close to the Smoky Mountain town.

"Yes, we were lucky—the winds shifted, and it faded out, but it's still very hot and dry here. And we have other issues now. A flu bug is going around and lots of people are sick. I sure know that I'm not feeling well."

"I hope you feel better soon!" Susan said from Brazil. "We could use a bit of your dry weather down here. It's been raining for the last few weeks. Hey, Alec, did you manage to get me the details on the steam engine?"

"Yes, sorry it took so long but I had to be away for a few weeks, here they are," he answered, and he went through the measurements and pieces that Epoch used for its small-scale steam engines.

"Thanks, Alec," Susan spoke animatedly. "This will save us a bunch of time in building one. We have so very few…"

Her voice became fragmented and their conversation was interrupted by loud static. A mechanical sounding voice that gave out a series of numbers stopped as suddenly as it started. Alec and the other operators were used to this intrusion, though none of them could explain it. The numbers appeared to be longitude and latitude coordinates to four locations, one of which was only a few hundred miles north of Epoch. The broadcast started some twenty years earlier and repeated a couple of times a day across key shortwave bands.

Although Epoch was close to one of the locations, it still took a few weeks to get there by horseback. Over the last decade, two trips had been made to the area to try and determine what was there. The first group came back after a few months having found nothing. The second group was never heard from again, and further attempts were prohibited until the technology existed to make the trip quicker. Alec and Jordan had decided that this was going to be one of the first things they explored when they finished their plane. They were eager to be the first people to figure out the radio-signal mystery.

2 - THE GREAT LOSS

Almost 200 years had elapsed since a virus had annihilated more than 99% of the world's population. Those left behind stayed resistant to its effects due to differences in their DNA structure. There were too few people to keep any kind of real technology going and very soon electrical grids, oil refineries and the like, went silent. The concepts of government, economics, and social structure collapsed, and for those that remained, it was a simple matter of survival.

With nearly all the human population gone, Nature went on a reclamation rampage and within this brief period had taken back much of what man had made. Modern structures crumbled to the ground, roadways disappeared under lush vegetation, and factories were transformed into not much more than rubbles of rusted steel overgrown with plants. Though forests expanded to near their size prior to the industrial revolution, vegetation was not the only thing that flourished. There was also an abundance of wildlife, such as wolves, deer, and bison that enjoyed the return to the natural order of things. Domesticated animals were not as lucky, and many were unable to survive the loss of humans providing food and shelter. Within the first decade, most perished, unable to adapt fast enough or compete for food.

Though there was no more pollution from factories and cars, the amount of greenhouse gases did not stop increasing when the Great Loss occurred. As the earth warmed, a threshold was reached where methane trapped in the northern permafrost was released, causing the amount of greenhouse gases to soar. All of this resulted in a significant heating of the planet, and in 200 years, ocean levels had increased twenty five to thirty feet, flooding all that remained of the major coastline cities and states worldwide. Rising sea levels was in no way an isolated issue. The high level of carbon in the air resulted in increased acidity of the water in the ocean. Much of the aquatic life could not adapt to this quickly enough, resulting in a near collapse of the ocean's food chain.

For the first few years after the virus, human survivors concentrated on scavenging for food by gathering dried or canned food that was prepared prior to the Great Loss. They were also able to use the abundance of already refined fuels such as gasoline and diesel. This allowed them to travel with ease and to use generators to power modern electrical appliances.

People found each other more by chance than anything else: spotting a campfire or a lighted building at night, hearing the crack of a rifle, or by the sound of a running generator or vehicle. Eventually, a group of a hundred people had gathered around what had been Spokane, Washington, and agreed that a long-term solution was needed. The refined fuel would soon decompose and become unusable, and the metropolitan area was becoming more dangerous with exploding gas lines, uncontrolled fires, and collapsing buildings. They decided to form a village outside of the urban areas where there would be good land for farming, proximity to a clean water source, such as a lake or river, and close to a source of ores for mining. They found these requisites within the interior of Washington State, and as an additional bonus found a recently drilled natural-gas well that had been capped near the prospective site.

Over a period of several of years, they used the large diesel and gas-powered bulldozers, cranes, and forklifts to build houses and roads and an enormous underground warehouse. The warehouse would store items not easily made that had been scavenged from hundreds of trips all over the country made in large semi-trailer trucks. During these trips, they found other small groups of people, and by the time they could no longer find useable fuel for their machines, their new village, Epoch, had a population of nearly 500 people.

In addition to the town, farms were set up and stocked with domesticated animals: cattle, horses, sheep, and chickens. They built large silos containing seed for various crops that they intended to grow. Roads were built into the forest for future logging operations and to an abandoned coal mine that was found about ten miles from the village site.

When the fuel was depleted, several large machines were placed in storage with the plan to use them when oil could be refined again. A few large machines were still needed though for farming and mining. After looking at several oil alternatives, such as bio-fuels and wood gasification, the villagers finally settled on making steam engines powered by the abundance of coal.

The natural-gas well did not prove as useful as they had thought it would. Without refinement, the gas contained several toxic chemicals and could not be used for either home heating or as a fuel for vehicles. However, it could be used to power a newly built steam-powered electricity plant.

The community became self-reliant with people learning to grow their own food, make clothes, and refine basic metalwork and forging skills. A simple economy was created with a currency established to allow for trading of goods and services, with the village acting like a central bank managed by an elected council and the town manager. The council and manager were responsible as well for the rationing of items from the warehouse and prioritizing the breakdown of work for centrally managed activities—farms, schools, mines, and mills.

Education in Epoch was different from the system employed prior to the Great Loss, with math, reading, writing, and history all covered by the age of twelve. Students who showed the highest aptitude and desire would take advanced studies at the Re-Discovery Center, which had been started to research now-forgotten technologies and manufacturing techniques. The Center was stocked with books obtained from many libraries around the country and had labs and workshops to test new ideas. During the first few decades, priority had been given to finding solutions for the mass production of simple things like nails, bolts, paper, and cloth. Research staff gradually increased, and the work progressed towards more complicated things with an emphasis on the petroleum-based technologies of drilling and the refinement of oil to make fuel, plastics, and rubber.

What the Re-Discovery Center lacked were computers. Without internet access, all the research had to be done by searching for and reading through books. There were computers set up initially to do basic computations and assist in the design of items, but problems appeared within the first few decades with components failing and the storage devices and media breaking down due to age. Without computers or internet, and with limited staff, the re-invention of new technologies was slowed almost to a halt. There were very few experts left in any field, and learning was acquired through what could be read in books or through trial and error.

There were additional hardships, including provision of enough food to meet Epoch's ever-increasing population. Without fertilizers, pesticides, and modern farm implements, productivity was much lower than the founders of Epoch had anticipated. Diseases in livestock and crops had led to chronic food shortages for the first several decades, especially during winter months. As the population grew, so did the problem. The DC was created to guard the nearby farms and warehouse against theft and from predators like the wolves that flourished in the new environment.

With the establishment of the DC and the discoveries of various fertilizers and pesticides, food issues were stabilized and allowed Epoch growth at a healthy pace. New businesses opened every year, and the combination of privately managed companies and those run by the council made for an agreeable environment. The council kept track of wages and the prices of items, and their influence ensured affordable food and housing for the average family.

Not everyone living in Epoch, however, shared a similar standard of living. Owners of well-run private companies, and those employed in positions of importance earned considerably more money than the average worker. These few could re-invest in new businesses and make even more money, and hence, renew a social structure like that before the Great Loss. A naturally developed echelon—the very wealthy being a small percentage of the population—and the majority working to afford shelter and food.

The growth of the Epoch did not come without setbacks. One hundred years following the Great Loss, fire destroyed one-quarter of the town. Rebuilding efforts slowed down other activities for several years and triggered rethinking of the water infrastructure. Epoch was located beside Skater lake, and initially, water for the community was simply pumped from the lake into a small filtration unit and then into homes. However, in emergencies; this system could not provide enough water as the pumps delivered a fixed quantity. To correct this, the council decided to build a large central water tower that would directly supply the town. .

Another setback came some fifty years after the fire when the natural-gas well, depended upon for electrical generation, began to run out. Without the technology to drill for and refine crude oil, a new electrical plant had to be made near a coal mine ten miles upstream and power lines extended into the village.

Despite the challenges, Epoch grew, and now, roughly 200 years after the Great Loss, the population count had reached ten thousand. The town had achieved the necessary critical mass to begin major expansion and develop more sophisticated machines to replace manual labor.

3 - RE-DISCOVERY

With great velocity, the broken spring flew to a corner of the lab, bounced off the wall, and landed on the floor near a few of its cousins that had met a similar fate.

“Do you feel better now, or do you want to throw another one?” Jordan asked.

“This is so frustrating," Alec replied. “We’ve been at this for weeks now, and always with the same result. The rest of the engine seems to be working fine, but these valve springs keep breaking."

They had been working for the last few months as one of several teams at the Re-Discovery Center concentrating on petroleum-based technologies. There were a few gasoline-powered engines stored in the warehouse, but their task was to create one from scratch and figure out how more could be manufactured rather than built by hand. Their plan was to start by building a small engine and then apply their findings to larger ones. They hoped to use the prototype engine in their plane since those in the warehouse were too big for the small aircraft.

Most of the engine development had gone well. They were lucky that besides the engines they could dismantle and examine in the warehouse, there were many books with detailed information on engine design. They alternated between the library and their lab to produce the pieces needed for the prototype engine, and they worked with village foundry and metalworkers on the best way to produce them. Some parts were particularly hard to get right since they needed specific alloy compositions to handle the rigorous demands placed upon them such as the valve springs.

They were just finishing up re-assembling the engine with a different set of springs when Allison and Kimberly showed up, each carrying a one-gallon can. “Hi, boys!” Allison said. “Still having problems?"

"Yeah, our new valve springs broke again," Alec said. He looked up and couldn't help thinking that Allison looked beautiful. She stood smiling at him, and he realized how lucky he was.

"New blend of fuel for us to try out?" Jordan asked as the girls set the cans down.

"Yes," said Kimberly, "and much better than the stuff we gave you last week. It's cleaner and has an octane count that will knock your socks off!"

"We're getting really close to finishing the refining process," Allison added, "and we're working with the other teams on plans for the refinery."

The re-introduction of oil in Epoch was going well. An old well had been found near the natural-gas well that the community had used, and Re-Discovery teams worked through the logistics of building a small drilling rig to put a new hole near it. Though not a gusher, oil had been found having a flow rate that would be more than enough for twice the current size of Epoch. With crude oil now available, there was a rush of activity towards refining it and making use of its products.

"Don't forget that the barbecue is only four days away," Allison said. "Both of you are still coming, aren't you?"

"Of course!" Alec replied, "and we'll bring a little surprise for you,"

"A surprise?" Allison said, "What are you two up to now?"

Alec shrugged. "You'll just have to wait and see, but I'm pretty sure you'll like it."

The girls looked at each other and knew they wouldn't get any more information. "Do you want to come with us for lunch? We're thinking of going to the greenhouse."

Alec and Jordan needed no further persuasion. They grabbed their lunch bags and headed out.

The greenhouse was a series of four large underground caverns positioned to form an X and having a small park and picnic area at its center. Built while the large machines were still operating, two of the caverns were kept at tropical temperatures and humidity allowing plants not native to the region to thrive. The other caverns were kept at a more moderate temperature for growing common vegetables.

Approaching the entrance of the greenhouse, they ran into two armed guards from the DC whose job was to ensure that entry stayed restricted to specific people. Jordan and Alec knew the guards, which sped up the validation of their Re-Discovery ID's. Once through the main doors, they walked down a long, downward-sloping hallway leading to the center of the greenhouse complex. Jordan and Kimberly decided to take a walk through one of the tropical sections while Alec and Allison found a spot on the grass in the picnic area.

"How's your plane project going?" asked Allison, knowing that Alec could talk indefinitely on the subject.

"Finding time to work on it is tough. We managed only one day last weekend because both Jordan and I were helping my dad on Saturday." He stretched out and locked his fingers behind his head. "We'll really have to buckle down if we want a hope at getting it done by fall. All of this depends on whether we can ever get that test engine to work. And yes, before you ask, you can be part of the second flight."

Allison grinned as she bent down and hugged him "As long as your first flight is with Jordan and not another girl." She laughed at his quizzical expression and snuggled up closer to him.

Near the end of their lunch break, Jordan and Kimberly returned, and the four bought an orange to split among them. "I'd love to live where we could grow these outside," Kimberly said, "but I guess that won't happen anytime soon."

“I wouldn’t say that so quickly," Jordan said. “Once we have the engines running and can start using other petroleum products, things will move faster. I think we’ll be able to start up satellite villages within the next ten years. The climate’s warming, and I’m guessing that we wouldn’t have to live too far south to grow oranges outside."

Kimberly smiled at the thought of being with Jordan at the start of a new community.

They started to head back, and as they were leaving the greenhouse, they ran into a thin young man pulling a wagon that contained some blemished fruits and vegetables that had been discarded.

“Hi, Clyde!” Jordan said

“Hey..." Clyde appeared glassy-eyed as he reached into his shirt pocket and proudly extended a hand that held an offering. “Want to try some of my new crop?”

Alec and Jordan looked around nervously to make sure that nobody was watching.

“Are you crazy, Clyde?” Jordan exclaimed. “That stuff is illegal; we could land a jail term for not turning you in."

“Chill man, nobody’s gonna bust us here. Do you do everything that HLFs tell you? Don’t you ever ask why occasionally?”

“HLFs?” Kimberly asked.

“The Higher Life Forms that run this little collection of people. The ones that make all the rules so that the elites can live better. People like him and his Dad," Clyde said accusingly, pointing at Alec.

“Hey!” Alec said. He started towards Clyde.

"Easy, man." Clyde said, stepping back. "I didn't mean to offend— just stating the facts is all. The system is what it is, and I don't agree with it, but I understand why most everyone plays along."

"And why is that?" Alec asked sarcastically.

"Hey, we'd have to smoke a few bowls to even scratch the surface on that. But, okay, for starters, the whole ownership-of-stuff thing is a key factor, and another is our hyper-individualism." Clyde leaned over his wagon and picked up an orange that had a large bruise on one side. He pointed to the piece of fruit that Kimberly was still holding.

"Why do we have to work so hard just for food and shelter, when food, except for the effort of growing and gathering, should basically be free." He whipped out a pocket knife, cut off the bruise, and offered the good part to Kimberly.

"Well, if you don't like it here, why not leave?" Alec challenged. "Nobody's going to stop you."

Clyde tucked the joint back into his pocket and smiled widely at Alec. "Our species is pretty social, and I like being around people. Plus, I feel compelled to try and do something to save you from yourselves."

Jordan could see that Alec was still angry. "Hey guys, we should get going—we're already running a bit late." He turned and slowly walked away.

Kimberly picked up the cue. "Yeah, see you later Clyde, and, uh, thanks for the orange." She ran a few steps to catch up with Jordan heading up the path back to the Re-Discovery Center.

"No problem," Clyde called after her. "I got it for free anyhow, and don't forget, if you ever want to sample my crop, just come on over." He picked up the wagon handle and started to leave.

Allison grasped Alec's hand and signaled him to leave. "I don't think that's going to happen anytime soon," she said.

"He's a bit creepy and has some pretty strange ideas," Kimberly said as she and Jordan returned to work. "Does he even have a job?"

"Well, creepy kind of fits him, that's for sure," Jordan said. "And as far as I know, he doesn't have a job. He lives in a small pre-Loss house a few miles from town and earns some money repairing and selling things that people throw out. Kind of a sad story from what I've been told. He was an only child, and there was some kind of accident when he was fifteen, killing both his parents. Maybe the combination of that and all the pot he smokes is the reason for his weird thinking. Hey, maybe we can develop some kind of drug to get him off of the pot and help him to start thinking straight."

"Maybe," she replied. "But there are only a few people working on drugs at Re-Discovery right now—and most of the effort is for heart issues that are on the rise."

Jordan nodded. He thought about his grandmother who had died the year before at the age of 71. She had joined an increasing number of people in Epoch whose deaths were due to heart disease.

It took a few days to refine the valve springs and final components for the engine. With the engine re-assembled, Alec and Jordan stood by the engine to see the results. "Gentlemen, start your engines," Jordan declared in a deep voice. He had learned the phrase from books in the library on racing and thought it was appropriate. He pressed the starter button, and the engine sputtered to life. After a few carburetor adjustments, it started to run more smoothly. When they increased the fuel, it ran well at about 1,000 rpm. During the next minute, they held their breath. They had not made it much further than this before, and as the engine ran longer and longer, they shouted with excitement and exchanged several high-fives.

This was the first time in 200 years that the planet had heard the sound of a gasoline engine running.

Word spread quickly throughout the Center, and soon the lab was full of people admiring their work. There was still a lot of testing to be done and modifications to make, but it was the best way to end the week, and they headed out to bask in their accomplishment.

"Do you have everything ready for the barbecue tomorrow night?" Alec asked Jordan as they rode the tram home.

"Yeah, we're all set. I hope that the girls and everyone else likes it."

Alec nodded. "You bet—I'm really looking forward to it—and to finally getting more time to work on the plane. See you tomorrow!" The tram came to a stop, and they jumped off and hurried to their homes.

As he walked in the front door, Alec was greeted with congratulations from his parents on getting the prototype engine working.

"How do you know about that?" Alec asked, "We just got it going a few hours ago."

"Well, word travels around this town pretty fast, especially with something as important as this," Jake replied. "Soon we'll have cars and trucks again, and we'll really be able to expand."

After supper that evening, Alec went down to the town hall for his radio shift. The usual group came online, and he was eager to fill them in on his accomplishments. He was about to begin telling them of the recent events when Brian came online from the Smoky Mountains and gave an update on the illness that had struck his town. His voice sounded strained.

"Good and bad news" The good news is that it looks like we don't have a flu bug, but we now know it's radiation poisoning that's causing everyone to be sick."

The radio went silent; only an occasional cough was heard.

"Where is it coming from?" Alec finally asked.

"The forest fire—it burned through a nuclear waste storage facility, and the heat must've weakened the cement. This won't end well. We've already seen dead animals and birds that had been downwind, and we're square in the middle of it. The doctors say there's little they can do after the dose we've had, and I fear most of us will be gone within a few more days."

Alec could hear the pain in Brian's voice and couldn't think of anything to say that didn't sound conciliatory He felt stunned as he listened to himself wish Brian the best. Then he shut off the radio and sat in silence, not yet believing that the whole town could be wiped out in a matter of days.

He continued to think about it the next morning when he and Jordan met at the shop to work on the plane.

"Wow—that's so sad." Jordan said after hearing the news.

"Yeah, the whole town. I wonder how many more of these storage sites are around and if any are close to here."

"I'm not sure," Jordan said. "I did some research on that a year or so ago, and there is one about a thousand miles east, but that's downwind so we wouldn't have to worry if it started to leak. The problem is the military stuff—a lot of data there was classified, so we don't know where it all is."

"I kind of understand the weapons thing," Alec said, "But I don't get the nuclear power generation angle. Why would they build these places knowing there'd be no safe way of dealing with the waste?"

Jordan shrugged. "Yeah, I can't figure that out either. But it was all about money and an energy-hungry population back then, and I guess they didn't care about what happened later."

They continued their work in silence for the rest of the morning. The basic structure of the plane was complete, and they worked on building up the control panel for the cockpit and the covering for the wings and body. They had found the gauges and many other hard-to-build items at the warehouse, but everything else needed to be hand-crafted.

Later in the afternoon, Alec looked up at the clock "We'd better get going to Kim's, or we'll need to build ourselves a large doghouse."

Jordan laughed. "Right—should be fun, though, and I'm looking forward to a good feed!" He put down his tools and then handed Alec a box that contained their surprise contribution to the event.

On their way over to Allison's, Alec started to laugh.

"What's so funny?" Jordan asked.

Alec pointed upward to the large DC recruitment poster that was painted on the side of a shop. Someone had changed the wording from "Join Now!" to "Light a Joint. Now!" and had painted a reefer hanging from the commander's lips.

"Dang, the commander is going to have a fit when he sees it," Jordan said, trying to suppress a laugh. "I like the old guy—who would do something like that?"

"But it's funny!" Alec said. He laughed loudly every time he looked at it.

When they arrived at Allison's house, they were startled by the crowd size. Usually, people were too busy to host or even attend this kind of gathering. There were a dozen families and several grandparents from the retirement home all engaged in conversation and games. Smoke from the barbecue pit drifted slowly outward leaving a mouthwatering aroma in its wake. People mingled in groups near the barbecue and at tables loaded with food.

Kim's antique record player was on display and provided music for people to listen to. When Alec saw Allison looking through stacks of old albums, he walked up quietly behind her and wrapped his arms around her.

"So you actually *did* manage to tear yourself away from the plane!" With obvious delight, she spun around and kissed him.

"Well—we were kind of hungry . . ." Alec began and was instantly interrupted by a sharp jab to his shoulder.

"So it was the food!" Allison said with mock outrage. "Okay, fine, but we didn't put all this together just so you could eat. Let's go over right now and talk to your grandma. She's been asking where you are." In a single fluid motion, she hooked her arm around his and led him towards a small woman who beamed when she saw him.

"She finally found you!" His grandmother put her hand up and stroked his face. Alec was happy to see her after several months, despite her constantly questioning him about when he might decide to get married.

"I want to have some great-grandkids to spoil, you know. Allison is such a lovely girl."

Allison loved the support and approval that the old woman openly displayed. She raised an eyebrow and glanced at Alec, who quickly diverted the conversation.

The afternoon went by rapidly and ended with a huge bonfire and Alec playing familiar songs on his guitar.

It was quite late when Kim prodded Jordan. "What was the big surprise that you've been talking about?"

Jordan looked at Alec, who shrugged "I guess it's as good a time as any," he said, and the two got up and retrieved the boxes that they brought. They began to remove the contents as Allison and Kim watched intently.

"Fireworks!" they said in unison. "Where did you get them?" Kim asked.

"We made them ourselves," Jordan said proudly. "Kind of a little side project. Now stand back, we haven't done much testing."

A crowd had gathered around, and Alec had them move back to a safer distance before he lit a fuse. A few seconds passed as the sparks hissed up the fuse and disappeared into the launch tube. Within a few seconds the firework shot out and erupted high in the sky into a shower of sparkling light. There were "oohs" and "aahs" from the crowd as the night sky continued to light up with explosions of bright colours and elaborate forms.

When the show ended, people began to leave, and Alec sat on the lawn and looked up at the sky. Allison rested against him. "The stars are so beautiful," she said stroking his arm.

"Yes, and it's a shame we don't do this kind of thing more often, but there never seems to be enough time. I sometimes wonder about what the purpose is of working so hard and not spending more time enjoying the here and now." As soon as his words were spoken, he thought about the conversation with Clyde a few days before. *Maybe he's on to something* . . .

4 - THE UNSEEN

Lauren sat by the creek having caught her fifth fish. She was awake while in meditation, acutely aware of her environment and the natural life within it. The rippling of the water and the chorus of songbirds were the only sounds that could be heard. She also sensed her old friend's presence nearby, and she smiled. Rather than putting her latest catch into her woven basket, she placed it on the rock beside her.

The wolf knew her intent, rose from the warm, sun-filled spot he had been lying in, and moved towards her to accept the offering. As he came close, she put her hand across his neck and caressed his soft fur. He paused, enjoying the attention, then took the fish and went back into the forest to return to his mate and cubs with an evening meal.

Even at a very young age, Lauren had shown uncanny abilities to interact with nature, whether plants or animals. She often wandered into the forest and was found a day later, unharmed, and wondering what all the fuss was about. At seven, she went missing for two days. The whole village searched for her, and she was finally found playing with two wolf cubs and their mother. She continued to visit them frequently, developing a special attachment to one of the cubs that came to be known as "Lauren's wolf." The two were a familiar sight walking through town together. Lauren's other differences became known and accepted— like her instinctive knowledge of herbs for medicine, and her ability to foresee future events.

As she watched the wolf disappear into the brush, Lauren wished that the moment would never end. She was startled by a crackling sound and hastened to open the flap on her pack. She pulled out a box, turned the dial, and pressed a button on the side. "This is Lauren, please repeat," she said.

"Hi, Lauren!" a voice replied. "Are you on your way back? I could use some fresh herbs for the stew I'm making."

She smiled at the sound of her mother's voice and wished that communication could also be exchanged through thought rather than dependence on technology. She pressed the button again. "Hi Mom, I'll be back by early afternoon—I was lucky and got four fish, and I can pick up some fresh parsley and oregano that I saw this morning."

The green light on the box turned red indicating that it had shut down for a while. She didn't understand why radios couldn't be made to last more than a few minutes before having to recharge.

She waded into the creek and gathered a few water samples in glass vials. Sealing them securely, she put the vials along with the rest of her belongings into her pack, picked up her day's catch, and set off in the direction of home, the village of Percipience.

Lauren entered her hut through the back door, which led into the kitchen. "Hi, Mom."

"Well, there you are—finally." Her mother glanced over her shoulder while stirring the contents of a pot on the stove. Several others helped with preparations for the evening meal.

"Here's my catch for the day and your herbs," Lauren said as she put the fish in the sink and the herbs on the counter. "I found some mushrooms; I think they'll go well in the stew."

"Sounds good, I'll use them right away. Dinner will be in a few hours, and I don't think we need any extra help so you can spend a bit of time down in the Research Center if you want."

"I think I'll do that. I need to drop off some water samples anyhow," Lauren replied. She picked up her pack and stealthily grabbed two cookies from the dessert dish without getting caught. Once outside, she walked by her clan's large garden, which consisted of a few acres of beans. Each of the clans in Percipience was responsible for growing specific items to be shared. There was little work to be done at this time of year, but later in the summer, there would be weeding and harvesting that the entire clan would help with.

She passed the garden and started down the path to the Lab, passing children playing catch and another group practicing their archery skills in preparation for The Games that were a month away. The kids spoke to each other in hushed voices as she walked by. She knew what they were saying.

"That's the girl that got banned from The Games."

"That's never happened before. Why? What did she do?"

She had heard it all before, and they were right—she could no longer compete in most of the events. The thought made her feel sad since she had looked forward to The Games as far back as she could remember. Now, because of who she was, she had been banished from most events for the rest of her life.

The Games were part of a large festival held at the village in spring and fall. The clans competed against each other in games of skill, strategy, and chance. Specific games and contestants from each hut were chosen by the elders, and everyone over the age of three had to participate in at least one event. The reward for the clan with the most winning points was a feast to be hosted and held by each of the other clans before the next game event. Selection of the competitors by the elders ensured that no one clan dominated the others and allowed everyone to enjoy the festival.

Lauren finally made it to the town center and passed by the town hall and outdoor auditorium. She opened the door to the Research Center and greeted her father, Robert, with a hug. "Here are your samples, Dad. I got four of them from different locations in the stream."

"Great, honey, do you have time to test them?" he asked.

"Sure." She had already spent a lot of time with her father in the Research Center. Like the Re-Discovery Center in Epoch, work was done here to relearn things from the time prior to the Great Loss, but unlike the Center, most of the work concentrated on new research in biology and chemistry.

Robert, like Lauren's late grandfather, felt passionate about sciences. In addition to developing a few drugs and chemicals for the village, he monitored rivers, creeks, and lakes in the surrounding area for toxic chemicals that seeped in from deteriorating storage facilities. She helped him gather water samples and if a toxic chemical was found they would head out to find the contamination source and see if there was a way stop it.

They worked together in silence for a brief time. "No sign of radiation," Lauren called out across the room. She made an entry in the log book.

"That's good." Her father looked pleased. "I wasn't expecting any, but you never know. Ever since our discovery, I worry more about the waterways to the west."

Several years earlier, a creek had been discovered carrying scores of dead fish and small animals. After tests, he had found high levels of radiation in the water, and later, with considerable effort, he found an old nuclear weapon storage facility upstream that had flooded. He had spent a few months at this facility with several people from the village diverting the water as best they could. As a long-term solution for weapons encasement, he was developing a type of cement that contained a high amount of lead.

"Did your radiation monitor pick up anything during your trip?" He pointed to a small device clipped to her backpack. The device emitted a sound and lit up when it detected radiation, and it was one of the precautions that everyone now took whenever going any distance from the village.

"Nope, not a beep," replied Lauren. She carefully measured a small amount of the water into a test tube and mixed in a few chemicals, comparing the resulting color to the chart. "There's a bit of mercury here," she said, showing the findings to her father.

“Yeah, like a few other creeks to the south of us,” he replied. “It's not good, but not horrible either. Way better than it used to be. Before the Great Loss, mercury levels were so high in most rivers that there was a restriction on the number of fish you could eat in a year without poisoning yourself."

“Ick...” She wrinkled her nose, already aware of the history. “I wonder where this is coming from—I’ve read that the biggest source used to be coal-fired power plants, but there are none around here."

“I’m not sure." He was sure he knew the source but didn’t want to tell her about it yet. “For now, I’m not going to worry too much about it—the levels are fairly low.” He changed the subject. “Hey, we should get going, or your mother will be annoyed if we’re late for the evening meal."

When they got back to their hut, Lauren went to the kitchen area to help with last minute preparations, while her father went to gather the children scattered about with their games. Once seated at the long table, everyone gave thanks to the earth for providing them with food and to the people who prepared it. The meal was simple, consisting mostly of vegetarian items and the fish that Lauren had caught. The pace remained leisurely, with people sharing stories from their day and their plans for the next.

After the meal, everyone scattered, with some heading to the town hall, which functioned as a social center, while others went to different clans to visit friends. Lauren walked to the river for her evening’s meditation, and Robert kept his commitment to be present at an elders’ meeting.

Lauren sat down near the river’s edge and looked out over the peaceful scene. The moon was almost full, and the stars blinked in their own nightly ritual. Although still young, she had been working on her meditation skills for more than ten years. It had seemed so natural a process to her, and she now able to focus quickly. She could disconnect from her emotions and concentrate on various energy flows around her. She felt the existence of other dimensions and universes and could sense past and future events. She tried to not focus too much on anything specific and worked more on achieving inner peace within her own universe.

This evening, however, she was having difficulty just as she had for the past several weeks. She felt premonitions of something bad that was about to happen and visions of things she couldn't explain. No matter how hard she tried, she couldn't get a clearer vision, and the more she worked on it, the more confused she became. Realizing it was of no use, she gave up. *When the time is right, I'll figure out what this is all about.* She headed up the moonlit path back to her hut.

The mood was solemn in the Elders Forum, a meeting room in the town center that was restricted to elders only. "It looks like Epoch is getting very close to getting their gasoline engine working," Robert announced. "I picked up chatter on the shortwave radio yesterday. They've also worked out most of the issues on petroleum refinement."

"We knew that this day would come, but it's much sooner than we expected," said one of the elders. Epoch had been detected some ten years after the Great Loss, and at that time, it was decided in the best interest of the Percipience not to let the rest of the population know. Exposure to the consumption-based society of Epoch would be to the determinant of the Percipience experience. When new members were brought into the group of elders, they went through a training period of several weeks, which included the sharing of the knowledge that Epoch did indeed exist.

Although there was no communication with Epoch, shortwave radios allowed Percipience to keep a close watch for news from there. To avoid detection from Epoch, the radios used around Percipience used encrypted signals and were modified to only work for a few minutes at a time. The excuse given was that they needed to recharge.

"With the engines and what is sure to be bigger earth-moving equipment, they'll be expanding more quickly," another elder added.

"It gets worse," Robert added. "A few of the young men there are working on an airplane, and it sounds like they're making good progress. With an aircraft, we'll be found quickly. We're going to have to start preparations and get the other elders involved." The rest of the group agreed and talked for several more hours about the work that needed to get done.

5 FIRST FLIGHT

"Explain to me how we got talked into helping these two work on this greasy, dirty project on our Saturday off," Kimberly asked. She crawled out from the back of the plane where she had been installing a second rudder-control cable.

"We'd never see them otherwise," Allison replied. "They've become obsessed with this over the last month." She knew this was probably an understatement. Throughout the winter, Alec and Jordan had spent countless hours of work on the plane. Now, as fall approached, they had devoted almost all their spare time to its completion.

"Did you need some help with that cable?" Jordan asked. He walked from his workbench with a newly built set of rails that would be used to mount the seats.

"It's already done," Kimberly said nonchalantly.

"Wow, cute *and* resourceful," he said, kissing her cheek.

She blushed slightly, took one of the rails from Jordan, and turned to go back to the plane. After only a few steps, she looked over her shoulder. "You just don't realize how much of both." Now it was Jordan's turn to blush, and the whole exchange made Allison laugh.

A loud shout came from outside the shed. They ran outside to find Alec sitting in a dirty puddle with most of him covered in mud. Allison rushed into the shed and came out carrying a camera and laughing as she quickly captured the image she was after. "This one will be priceless," she said, "I can hardly wait to see how it turns out."

The camera had come from the warehouse, and the film inside was one of the newest products from the Re-Discovery Center—one of the many items re-appearing as research in plastics continued. The ability to visually record daily life in Epoch was a high priority of the people and village council. Film was among first things completed, and only a few rolls had been created as prototypes. Full-scale production would be accessible with the new factories opening online, timed to coincide with the pending completion of the refinery.

Jordan looked around trying to figure out what happened. "What were you trying to do?" he asked.

Alec pointed down the slope to the lake. The reserve fuel tank that he been carrying bobbed along in the water. "I slipped coming down," he said running his hands through his mud-soaked hair. "We didn't really need a reserve tank anyhow, right?"

Jordan was already at the water's edge to retrieve the tank. Allison and Kimberly cleaned off Alec as he got to his feet. He pulled Allison into an embrace that assured an equal transfer of mud at the same time. "Aghhh…you're so bad," she said, looking at her dirt-spattered clothes.

"Just a little payback for taking that picture." Alec replied. "We'd better get back to it— we're so close now."

"We would've been finished two weeks ago if it hadn't been for your mom," Jordan said as he approached carrying the dripping fuel tank. "All we've been doing for the past few weeks is adding things that she has been suggesting for safety such as this reserve fuel tank and redundant control cables."

"Yeah, now that we're getting close, she's getting worried," Alec commented. "But I have to agree that most of her ideas have been good ones. I think this reserve fuel tank is the last of them, though, and to make sure that it is let's get it in quickly and get that plane in the water."

"Agreed," Jordan said. "And then we'll call it done. Why don't you and Allison put the tank in, and Kimberly and I'll head up to Re-Discovery and get a few cans of fuel."

"Good plan," Allison agreed. "I don't want to be seen like this anyway."

"Hey, while you and Kimberly are up there, try to recruit some help," Alec said. "We could use more people to get the plane down to the lake. And on your way, check out the latest DC recruitment poster on the bank's wall. Someone touched it up last night."

"Will do," Jordan said as he and Kimberly cautiously walked back up the muddy slope.

Alec and Allison went back into the shed. "What's on the poster this time?" she asked.

"Well, the original poster looked like most, with a picture of the commander and the slogan, 'I Need You!' underneath it, someone added sunglasses, a drink in the commander's hand, and the words, 'To Relax' on the bottom."

She giggled. "I've *got* to see that before they remove it. I wonder who did it. They have to be pretty good not to get caught."

"Yeah," said Alec, "but I know the commander isn't laughing."

They finished fitting the reserve fuel tank in the plane, and then mounted the rear door and stepped back to admire the finished product.

"I can't believe it's finally finished!" Alec said, wrapping his arm around her waist.

He recalled that very few people thought it would ever actually get done. Fully loaded with fuel, the plane would fly around 300 miles before having to return. It was a two-seater with a closed cockpit and a small cargo area with two folding seats. If needed, two extra people could be carried as human cargo.

"It's beautiful," she said as she snuggled in closer to him, "Are you sure that you and Jordan have to do the first flight?"

"You'll go up with me soon enough, but we're not taking any passengers on the first run."

The large sliding door to the shed opened, allowing the bright, warm sunshine to invade the building.

"We're back!" Jordan said. "Along with a few people to help out."

Unruly lines of people crowded into the shed. "How many people did you find?" Alec yelled over the noise of excited voices.

"I think there are at least fifty," Jordan shouted back. "It was easy—everyone wants to see this."

"OK, let's make use of them all," Alec said. "We need people to clean up the shed, and others to help set up the rollers we've got outside." He noticed a figure in the crowd. "Hey, Clyde! What are you doing here?"

"Hey, pretty cool, plane man. I was kind of curious, and I figured there'd probably be some good scrap metal you'd be throwing out that I could use." He looked at the plane approvingly. "Do you mind if I look inside?"

Alec wanted to say no, but didn't want to risk starting a scene with so many people around. "I guess—just don't touch anything,"

"Sure, man. Thanks." Clyde made his way to the rear door of the plane.

With all the help on hand, it didn't take long to clean the shed enough to give the plane a clear path to the door. Logs were moved to act as rollers, and with the added help of a few jacks, they were able to raise the plane. The move went slowly along the fifty yards between the shed and the lake. As the plane rolled off one log after another, replacements were repeatedly carried to the front until they reached the edge of the water.

The mood had become one of shared celebration, and a last bit of effort included everyone wading through the cool lake water. The plane made its long-awaited departure from land and floated on the surface of the lake. A cheer rose into the air, and Allison shot various pictures of the historic event.

The plane was easy enough to pull over to the newly built floating dock. Jordan and Alec made sure it was well secured, and Kimberly and Allison brought the fuel cans. The sun was setting, and the whole operation had taken much longer than expected.

“Let’s gas it up tonight," Jordan said, “I don’t want to do anything tomorrow except get in and go."

“I’m with you, but you’ll have to wait until after Allison and I get out of church," Alec said.

“Do you have to go?” Jordan moaned, “Can’t you skip it just this once?"

“Not a chance," Alec replied, “Unless I want to move out of my parents’ house. My dad is fanatical about me attending.”

“Well, we’ll be waiting for you here whenever you and Allison get sprung."

The only thing that kept Alec from dozing off during church service the next morning was Allison’s jabs to his ribs. Like a kid on Christmas Eve, he had hardly slept at all in anticipation of the next day’s activities, and the service offered little to keep him awake.

Allison’s last jab had been particularly hard. He looked at her reproachfully, but she only rolled her eyes and smiled apologetically. The service seemed longer than usual as the pastor spoke about the importance of faith and quoted numerous biblical verses. Alec focused for a moment on what was being said:

“... and from Hebrews 11:1 “Now faith is the assurance of things hoped for, the conviction of things not seen.” And from Ephesians 2:8 “For by grace you have been saved through faith. And this is not your own doing; it is the gift of God..."”

I have faith in science, what I can see, measure, and understand. He thought about the sermon from several weeks earlier about evolution versus creation. The pastor had preached that humans were not only made in God's image but created within the last 10,000 years. *This in the face of scientific evidence that proves we evolved like everything else on the planet.*

Alec thoughts were interrupted by the sound of shuffling feet, and he realized the service was over. Eager to get to the plane, he coaxed Allison to move along, not noticing the person beside him as they made their way to the exit.

"I'm surprised to see you here today, Alec," Clyde said. "I'd have bet on you skipping out so that you could get into that plane."

"Wouldn't miss all this for the world," Alec said sarcastically. He didn't feel like chatting with Clyde and gave Allison another nudge.

"Yeah, man, I look forward to them, too," Clyde said, seemingly unaware of Alec's mocking tone.

Alec tried to hold back but was unsuccessful. "You actually believe this stuff? There can't be more than a dozen people our age here, and I think most have been forced by their parents."

Clyde glanced around and saw that what Alec said was correct. "Too bad," he said. "Look, I get the whole science-versus-religion thing, but I think most people are missing the point here."

"And that is?" Alec said, taking the bait.

"The point is that the church, or rather most religions, in general, help us with our moral compass. They give us a sense of right and wrong while not trying to explain every little thing. After all, we need some mystic and magic in our lives, don't we? It would be pretty darn boring if we understood everything."

The door was a few feet away, and Alec was now barely listening to Clyde. "Through science we have a good understanding of everything," he said.

Clyde grunted. "Oh, is that so? If science can't explain something, then it probably doesn't exist and gets ridiculed—like the people who believe in déjà-vu, telepathy, or even in an all-powerful being like a god."

Alec thought back to the night he held a wolf in his rifle sights and could have sworn that the animal knew his intentions. There had been no way he even could have been heard. He also remembered the dog that he sensed had been watching over him, and Koda's strange behavior the day he returned from the DC. But then the thoughts evaporated as he finally stepped through the Church door into the daylight. He left quickly with Allison, leaving Clyde talking to the air.

As they made their way to the lake, almost the entire congregation followed them. At the halfway point, Alec's mother caught up with the speeding pair.

"Now Alec, you'll be careful—no silly risks today, do you hear me?"

"Yes, Mom. You have nothing to worry about today. We're just going to fire it up and practice a few runs across the lake to see how it handles. We'll be checking everything, and if all looks good, we'll take it into the air tomorrow."

"I know how spontaneous you can be, dear, just not today, ok?" She didn't tell Alec that for the last month, she had felt a premonition that something bad was going to happen. The feeling was more than a mother's concern for her son; to her it was a forewarning, and she had been after Alec and Jorden to make the plane as safe as possible.

"Yes, Mom, we'll take it easy."

"For once, I agree with your mom," Allison said. She slid her arms around his shoulders. "Please be careful."

"We'll be fine," Alec said. "Hey, can I borrow the camera for this trip? I want to take a few pictures of our first excursion."

She handed him the camera, and Alec took his first step onto the dock. He knew that both his mother and Allison were worried, but he and Jordan had done a significant amount of testing on every component of the plane, most especially on the engine. The engine prototypes had gone through thousands of hours of testing and tweaking. They had torn them apart to observe wear patterns, changing things where necessary. They had stress-tested cables and as much of the structure of the plane as they could without getting it into the air.

For the last several years, the dream of flying had been an obsession for both, and they had learned as much as they could about flying planes from the books in the Re-Discovery library. Everything from general principals of flying and navigation to how to handle mechanical emergencies. They also spent time studying how weather impacted flight and what to expect under different conditions. Without actually flying, they both felt as ready as they would ever be.

When Alec reached the plane, Jordan had already untied the ropes. They had flipped a coin the day before to see who would be first behind the controls. Jordan had won.

"You ready for this?" Alec asked.

"I guess—just getting used to this being real now. We've been working on it for so long," Jordan said. "We couldn't have asked for a better day. There's been no wind this morning."

Alec looked across Skater Lake and could see barely a ripple. The sky was a cloudless blue.

"Couldn't agree with you more. Where's Kimberly?"

"She left a while ago. Said she forgot something and that she'd be back in a bit." Jordan looked through the crowds on the lakeshore. "There—I see her." He pointed as she made her way through the crowd and reached the dock.

"I can't believe I almost forgot these," she said, proudly holding up two sets of aviator sunglasses.

"Cool," Jordan said as he reached for a pair.

"Did you have these made?" Alec asked.

"No, I found a small box of them in the warehouse about six months ago while doing inventory and had stashed them away for just this moment."

Alec and Jordan donned the sunglasses and Kimberly took a picture of them under the wing of the plane. She put her arms around Jordan. "Be safe," she said, then turned to Alec. "And don't do anything crazy like trying to fly today. Remember—just across the lake and back a few times, and that's it."

He put on his best hurt look. "When have I ever done anything spontaneous?" he asked.

Kimberly pointed a finger in mock accusation and moved back to join the rest of the crowd.

Jordan climbed into the plane and crossed to the pilot's seat. "Showtime!" he said. Alec followed and settled into the co-pilot side. Knowing that his mother would be paying close attention, he fastened his seat harness with deliberately exaggerated movements before closing the door.

"Okay, let's see if we did a good job or whether we'll have to take a long swim back here," Alec said. After completing pre-flight checks, he hit the starter button and watched as the propeller began to slowly rotate. The engine started immediately, and Jordan brought the throttle down quickly as the plane began moving. He let his breath out slowly as he pushed up on the throttle. The aircraft pulled away from the dock.

A crackling sound erupted from the speaker. "Hi, boys!" Just doing a quick radio check," Allison said.

"Roger that," said Jordan. "We hear you loud and clear. Talk to you from the other side!" He laughed imagining her reaction.

The plane moved effortlessly across the water, and Jordan practiced turning left and right at a slow speed. "So far, so good." He pointed the nose towards the opposite side of the lake and pushed the throttle up to one-quarter power. They lunged forward, which shocked them slightly, but everything remained stable. As the plane began to pick up speed, they clapped hands in a high-five salute, thrilled by the feeling of the speed across the water. They reached three-quarters of the way across Skater Lake before Jordan eased the throttle, and the plane instantly slowed.

"This thing really moves, and we weren't even close to lift off speed," Jordan said.

"I know—I've never moved that fast before," Alec replied.

"Allison, can you hear us?" Jordan said into the microphone.

"Yes, is everything OK? We can hardly see you."

"Everything's fine—and boy does this crate move!"

The plane had slowed to a crawl, and Jordan turned it around. "Okay, your turn."

They switched places, and Alec throttled the engines once again, first practicing turning in the open water and then shooting across the lake towards Epoch. Their speed was faster this time but still not near enough to the takeoff requirement. Jordan followed the different gauges on the instrument panel and took notes.

“Looks pretty good," he said. He watched Alec cut back on the throttle, and they slowed down. “Getting good readings from the engine, and it looks like the airspeed gauge is working too, at least at these slow speeds."

They had worried about the difficulty in calibrating the airspeed gauge, even with the makeshift wind tunnel that they had built for it. They traded places again.

“This time I'm going to have a run with the water rudders left up and increase the speed a bit more," Jordan said.

“Your call, but yeah, if you watch the speed, we should be ok," Alec said.

Jordan turned the plane around and brought the speed up to where the wings could nearly produce enough lift to fly off the water. The engine no longer had to force its way through the water, and the plane immediately veered to the left. Jordan felt caught off guard but quickly recovered and adjusted the yoke.

As they sped across the lake, they became consumed with guiding the plane and monitoring the instrument panel. They were half way across the lake when Alec looked out of the window and then down at the floats.

“Uh... Jordan . . .”

“What?" Jordan kept his eyes looking forward.

“We're really flying!" Alec exclaimed. His words rushed together. “We're about five feet above the water right now."

“No way!" Jordan said. He looked out his window and saw the floats above the water then looked out of the front window. “Wow—with the water being so smooth it's hard to tell that we're a few feet up. That airspeed gauge must be off . . . we shouldn't be at takeoff speed yet."

“Alec! What are you doing?" Allison's voice sounded shrill.

Alec picked up the microphone. "Hey, Jordan is flying—and it was an accident!"

"So what do we do now—try to land or take it up?" Jordan asked.

"Bring it down, Alec!" Allison said, her voice shaking. "From what we can see, you're nearly across the lake and don't have much time left."

"She's right," Jordan said. He pushed the throttle up and pulled back gently on the stick. The plane responded to the new freedom and climbed smoothly and quickly.

"I guess it's decided," Alec said. "Right now, we're safer at a higher altitude, so take it up a bit more." He picked up the receiver. "Allison, we're a bit busy now, but I'll get back to you in a couple of minutes."

Jordan nodded and pulled back more on the stick. The plane responded eagerly, creating a queasy sensation in their stomachs. They were soon a few hundred feet above the trees on the far side of Skater Lake. Feeling more confident, Jordan moved the stick lightly, and the plane responded and banked easily to the right.

"We did it!" Alec said, momentarily forgetting the predicament that they were in.

"Yeah," Jordan said. He felt more relaxed and continued to bank the plane until they were heading towards Epoch. They were no longer climbing and flew steadily at five hundred feet above the water. As they neared the shoreline, they could see crowds of people waving at them. Alec fished inside his coat pocket, removed the camera, and took several pictures of everything he could see below him.

They continued for a few minutes past Epoch before turning around to head back to the lake.

"Allison, you still there?"

"Yes!" she answered loudly, "What are you guys doing? You've scared us all to death down here!"

"We're coming back now and will try to land. If things don't look or feel right, we'll bring it back up and try again. And you can beat me up in person in a few minutes."

"You can bet on that!"

As they neared the lake, Jordan throttled down, and the plane began to descend. They flew over the crowds again, this time at a lower altitude. Within minutes, only twenty feet of air remained between them and the lake. Jordan cut the power and pointed the nose above the horizon, and soon he could feel the floats touching the water. He pulled back as hard as he dared, hoping that the floats wouldn't get caught in the water, causing them to flip over. His fears were unfounded as the plane leveled itself and began to glide across the lake.

"Jesus!" Jordan said with relief.

"What a rush—that was a perfect landing. I hardly felt a thing!" Alec said.

Jordan pushed the throttle up, engaging the water rudders and guided the plane back to the dock. There was a flurry of commotion. Some people tried to secure the plane, and others tried to reach Alec and Jordan to scold them for their recklessness, and at the same time, congratulate them on their successful flight.

After the initial pandemonium had died down, Jordan admitted that he was at the controls through the flight and that even he hadn't realized they were in the air until Alec had informed him. Both Allison and Alec's mother looked relieved at this news as they joined the excited chatter.

Though the flight put Alec and Jordan to celebrity status all over Epoch, there was also big pressure on them from both Alec's father and the DC's Commander for aerial reconnaissance of Epoch's outlying area. Since the disappearance of petroleum fuel nearly two centuries earlier, little was known of the world beyond a fifty-mile radius outside Epoch. The commander wanted to know if there were other major towns that could pose a threat to Epoch while Jake needed information about old villages or factories that might be reached to scavenge much needed resources, like copper.

"Our oil refinery won't be online till late fall," Jake told the commander during one of their heated debates, "and until then, we'll be able to make enough fuel to fly this contraption only once every few weeks."

"Which is exactly why we should fly out to the coast," the commander said. "If there are other surviving population centers close by, that's where we'll find them."

Jake challenged that idea. "Maybe. But even if we did, we'd have to cross at least five rivers, and all the bridges crossing them would have surely collapsed by now. There's a much closer town that existed just over a hundred miles north of here. Re-building a road to that point would be much easier, and then we'd have access to lots of scrap material. May I remind you that all the plans you put in for military vehicles will require that scrap material to build?"

The commander conceded the point. "I guess the trip to the coast must wait a few more months, but after that I insist that we start the grid search of surrounding areas." He was furious as this was the second time that he had been out maneuvered by Jake. The previous fall, Jake had gone behind his back and got the funding for the DC cut directly after he had lobbied to get it increased. He believed that Jake was growing too powerful and that he would soon have to do something about this.

With nothing else to say, the commander made his way out of Jake's office.

"Don't forget to relax!" Jake shouted after him.

The commander turned to face Jake, his face reddening with anger. "When I catch whoever is behind that graffiti crap, I'll have them flogged in the town center," he said, and stormed out of the office.

Jake looked down at his paper work and gave up maintaining a straight face. He couldn't help relishing the added aggravation he was causing the commander.

6 - THE GAMES

There was a great deal of excitement in Percipience the evening before the opening of the fall Games. Most of the village congregated around the town hall to read the competition list and see who the contestants would be in each event. In an open area nearby, there was a group of fifty large tents, one from each of the clan huts that were to be used the next day as gathering points during The Games. Each tent presented a specific delicacy, and people walked from tent to tent to sample food, listen to music, and size up the competition that they would face the following day.

Lauren had spent several days helping to prepare the large amounts of cornbread and chili that were her clan's contribution to the evening's feast.

"Ready for tomorrow?" a young man asked as she loaded his bowl with chili.

"I hope so." She tried to sound at least a little excited and wondered why he looked familiar.

"Did you check the competition list?" he asked. "I'm going to be in The Run with you tomorrow. Maybe we can have a repeat of last fall when we came in first and second."

His tall, slender body and bearing triggered Lauren's memory. She couldn't remember his name, but felt sure that he shared antelope DNA when recalling his running speed and grace. He had placed first, a full ten minutes before she came through in a distant second place.

He's in even better shape now. I don't have a hope. She cut off a piece of corn bread to go with his chili. *Still, if I come in second, it'll give my clan a good amount of points."*

"Well, we'll have to see how it goes," she said with a forced smile. "See you tomorrow!"

She had always looked forward to The Games. Now, though still fun, they had lost most of their excitement for her since she had been forbidden to compete in all but The Run.

The event consisted of a grueling fifteen-mile trek to the top of a small mountain, taking the clan flag that had been placed there for each competitor, and racing back to the town hall. It was by far the longest event of The Games and took the entire day to complete. The elders had chosen it for her since they needed to know that she was nowhere near the other competitions.

For the elders, the purpose of the games was more than just a festival and a way to start the spring planting and fall harvest. The Games were used by them to judge people's strengths and weaknesses for the genetic pairing program. The process had been proven to work well for decades but became problematic a few years ago, and they had isolated the source of the problem—Lauren.

It began when Lauren had been working on improving her archery skills for The Games. She was starting to find success by going into a near meditative trance while shooting her arrows and urging them to find their mark. With refinement, she eventually found that she could fire arrow after arrow and hit the bull's-eye each time. She also noticed that she could control, to a noticeable degree, other physical phenomena like walking through the rain and not getting wet. The elders quickly realized that not only was she influencing her own events, but any that she watched others compete as well, to the point where they could no longer fairly judge the abilities of other competitors.

Lauren protested strongly when she learned of her being forbidden to compete in nearly all the events. She pointed to a few other events that she could participate in; for instance, the limbo. But the elders would not be swayed and remained adamant. She would have to stay away from The Games so that her influence, even as a spectator, would not affect anyone competing.

Within their inner circle, however, the elders were elated by Lauren's abilities. Others within Percipience had shown weaker signs of similar skills, but nothing close to what Lauren demonstrated. They saw this as proof that their plan was on the right track. When Percipience was being established, their benefactor had given them the formula for a substance they were instructed to introduce into their food. Given several generations and selective pairings of parents, he explained that it would improve cognitive abilities to the point where psychic abilities like telekinesis would be possible. Lauren was proof that he was right.

Robert passed by as Lauren was about to end her shift in the food line. "Are you heading out for a meditation break or going back to our hut?" he asked.

"I was going to meditate," she said, "but I've been having problems with that lately. Can we talk about it?"

"Of course, honey", he replied. "I was going back to the hut—I need to get to sleep early so that I'm rested for my competition tomorrow."

"What did you get selected for?"

"Nothing glamorous this year. I got the Hemp Harvest," he said.

Lauren laughed and squeezed her father's arm. "That's better than The Run."

The Hemp Harvest involved teams of two people from each clan who were given a section of the local hemp field to cut and wrap into bundles. The first team to finish won and the judges deducted points for poorly tied bundles or unnecessary wastage.

"Why don't we chat on the way back?" her father asked.

She linked her arm through her father's, and they started along a path that snaked its way through the trees.

"What's on your mind?"

She found it hard to begin. She rarely talked about her meditation sessions since nobody ever seemed to understand what she was experiencing.

"I've been having visions lately that I don't understand. Normally, I don't get too concerned about them, but they're getting more intense. And with them comes a sense that something very terrible is about to happen." Her father's face showed his concern.

"What kind of visions?" He wondered if this could be about Epoch.

"That's the thing— they don't make any sense. I see a pyramid, a white pyramid in a forest, and there are vehicles and some kind of big conflict and sadness. It might all be from the past, but usually I can tell, and I'm not getting that feeling now."

"A pyramid? Like the ones we've seen in the books about Egypt?"

"Kind of, but it appears to be much smaller, and it's among trees and hills, not in the desert," she said. "It's not the pyramid that's bothering me, though; it's the overwhelming sense of conflict and loss that I sense. Just when it feels too overwhelming, it disappears, and I come out of it."

"I'm not sure what to say," her father said thoughtfully. "The pyramid must represent something, but I doubt we'll be able to figure it out until something actually happens. I know that your abilities will take you deeper into meditation than anyone else in Percipience. You remind me of the shamans I have read about that existed among the native North Americans." He put his arm around her shoulder and drew her close to him. "I'm afraid that I can't be of much help, but I'll bring it up at the next elders' meeting so that every hut will be on the watch for anything unusual."

They walked without speaking for the rest of way. When they entered their hut, he noticed there were people already back from the evening festivities. He looked at his daughter with affection. "I don't know what to suggest, but I do know that you mustn't give up. There is some reason for this happening, and it may be important for you to figure out what's going on."

"I know, Dad," Lauren replied, "Just talking about it has helped. I'll keep trying and let you know how it goes."

"Good." Robert said, hugging her. "Now, I need to give this old body some sleep, and I think you could use more rest too."

"Yeah, you're right, good night, Dad," She kissed her father and went to get ready for bed.

Robert watched as she walked away and felt a shiver run through his body. Deep inside, he knew with certainty that Lauren was picking up something from their future and that it was related to Epoch. None of it sounded like it would go well.

Lauren and several others from her hut were awakened the next morning to strange sounds coming from close by. She got up from her sleeping mat and went outside. Her father was making another attempt to get some noise out of a large didgeridoo but was rewarded by the same unrecognizable sound.

She giggled out loud. "Is there a moose out here?"

He shook his head while holding the long, bamboo instrument. "I could never get the hang of these things," he said.

"Well, I'd stop now if I were you unless you want to attract every predator within miles that might be looking for that wounded moose."

"It was that bad?" He laughed and flung down the instrument in mild frustration.

Lauren nodded and then heard a few other distant didgeridoos.

"That's how it's supposed to sound," she said.

Playing the didgeridoos at first light on the day of The Games was a tradition started a few decades before. All the clans participated, and the noise continued for at least half an hour. It was not a particularly popular instrument, and one that required practice to master, but it was an entertaining start to the day as people tried to create a musical sound.

After a quick breakfast, the clans headed down to the village center. The Run was the first event as it took the longest. Lauren made her way to the starting area and lined up with runners from other clan huts including the young man who had spoken to her the day before. He nodded and smiled when she arrived.

Did his legs get longer overnight?

Without much ceremony, one of the judges gave the start signal, and the contestants sprinted off. They clustered together in the beginning, but that would soon change as everyone had their own secret path to the top of the mountain.

At the center of town, there continued well-organized chaos with people going in every direction to either compete in or view an event. The more popular events, like archery, dodge ball, and the limbo, were held in the village center, while many of the smaller events like board games, frog racing, and cooking, were hosted at various clan huts.

Though most of the events were arranged for competition, there were practical purposes behind some of them. During the spring games, there was a hemp-seed planting competition and hemp harvesting in the fall games. The cooking competitions guaranteed plenty of things to eat during the day, and the music competitions supplied entertainment for all. Large bonfires were kept blazing to add to the festival mood.

Lauren thought she made it in good time to the top of the mountain, but when she got there, she was disappointed to see that two other runners had already claimed their clan flags. Discouraged, she decided to take a short break to catch her breath and admire the scenery. She could see parts of

Percipience below, and her gaze followed the river into the forested rolling hills. She saw larger mountains to the east and west and more forest to the north and south.

She was about to start back down when she noticed a speck in the southern sky. It was too far away to clearly see what it was, but she knew it wasn't a bird. It flew in a straight line then dipped and climbed to the same altitude as before. *Could it be?* She had only read about planes in books, but there was no other explanation for what she was seeing. Others too had seen moving lights in Percipience's night sky, but they had been from meteors. This was daytime, and she could sense that it wasn't a natural occurrence. After observing the speck for a while, and now, with a renewed sense of purpose, she seized her clan's flag and began a quick descent down the mountain.

Despite a reckless pace faster than she had run before, she came in second by the time she reached the finish line. Nonetheless, she brushed past the applauding crowd waiting to congratulate her and ran straight towards her father who was helping to tabulate the incoming scores.

"Dad! Dad! I saw a plane when I was on top of the mountain," she said, still short of breath.

A few people nearby heard what she said and turned to follow the conversation. Her father immediately put his arm around her and guided her away from the score booth.

"A plane? Are you sure?"

"Yes, there's no way that this was a natural thing." she said. She struggled to catch her breath and then described what she had seen. Her father showed less surprise than she had expected, and she was equally surprised at his next question.

"Did they see you?"

"Uh, no... I don't think so. It was pretty far away." She felt perplexed by her father's question and lack of reaction, "Dad, it was a plane. Do you know what this means? There are other towns out there and probably close by."

"OK, let's talk about this after The Games tonight. Don't tell anyone about this."

"But Dad! It was a plane ..."

"I heard you the first three times, and I believe you, but we need to talk about this in private later." His tone made it clear that she was to listen and do as he asked.

She wandered back into the crowd, confused and excited at the same time. She had lost track of The Games, and that her placing in the race had helped her clan by putting them only a couple of points behind the leading hut. There was still one event left, which was a board game between her grandmother and a five-year-old from the leading hut.

She arrived just as the five-year-old boy won. She witnessed a perfectly fabricated outrage by her grandmother, much to the delight and laughter of the crowd that had been watching. The winner was hoisted up by two people from the winning hut. A spontaneous parade made its way to the village center for the feast and bonfires that awaited them. Though the festivities went late into the evening with music and dancing, Lauren felt out of place. Still puzzled by her father's reaction, she also thought about what it would mean if there *were* another town close by, and one obviously more advanced.

She was deep in thought as she watched the flames in the bonfire dance to the music. Her father tapped her shoulder. She looked up and saw his reassuring, calm smile.

"Let's head over to the Research Center," he said. "We can talk better if we're away from all of this." He made a sweeping gesture to the people and noise surrounding them.

She nodded and followed him to the Center, noticing that he locked the door as soon as they had entered. They walked down a hallway and let themselves into a meeting room. She sat opposite her father at a small conference table.

"I'm sure you have lots of questions about what you saw today," he said, "and I'm sorry I acted the way I did. You caught me off guard, honey, so let me explain a few things." He began with his agreement with the elders to keep information about Epoch and its progress in secret from the rest of Percipience.

She felt more shocked by this revelation than by her sighting of the plane. For a few seconds, she sat dumbfounded and could think of nothing but having been lied to her entire life. None of her thoughts made sense to her, and all she could feel was a surge of anger spilling over her.

"Why would you do such a thing? Are there other villages or secrets I still don't know about?"

"At the time of the Great Loss there were four villages like ours. Paradise, Pellucid, Provenance and us. We're not exactly sure what happened to two of them, but we keep in regular contact with Provenance, which is in Australia. However, there are no other villages like Epoch even remotely close to us that we know of," her father said quietly. "But you have to understand why this was kept from you. Our way of life and that of Epoch's simply can't coexist."

"Why not—what makes you so sure?"

He knew she was angry but felt she needed to realize the consequences of the two cultures merging. "Societies more technologically advanced have always assimilated those with lower levels of technology. And the flaw isn't in technology—it's in the consumption and economic patterns that drive them to expand. The technology just allows them to do it more easily. Maybe they *can* coexist, but so far in recorded history, it hasn't worked out."

She tried to absorb all that her father had said despite her angry confusion "So what's going to happen to us now?"

He played distractedly with a piece of paper that was left on the table as he listened to the concern in her voice. "I'm sure they'll discover us soon, but the elders and I have been discussing plans to break the historical pattern of domination." He raised his hand before she could ask another question or offer an objection. "I'm sorry I can't tell you more, but we're keeping things to ourselves right now. The rest of the village will find out all at the same time."

She started to stand, and he reached over and took hand. "Lauren, I need you to not tell anyone about what you saw today or any part of what I've told you. The truth will come out soon enough, and we don't need people panicking or running off and doing things on their own."

She still couldn't take in all the information. Percipience had been the center of her world. She had learned about Earth before the Great Loss and believed there could be other villages out there but had assumed they would be like Percipience. How could they be different—and what was the "consumption and economics" that her father talked about?

"Okay, I guess." She didn't know what else to say.

They stood up, and her father hugged her. "Don't worry, honey. Things will work out."

Lauren returned his hug sensing that her father needed it more than she did.

They left the Center, and Robert returned to the celebrations while Lauren wandered down to the river. Raw emotions steered her thoughts, and she knew that nothing could be sorted out until she regained control of herself.

She could still hear the music from the festival as she settled by the river bank. After a few minutes, she sensed something behind her. She smiled and laid her hand out and was immediately rewarded with the nuzzling of a wet nose followed by the feel of thick fur. Her wolf moved in closer, and she knew that his coat was already thickening in preparation for winter. She felt as much comfort running her hands through it as the wolf did from the affectionate attention. As the moon broke through the clouds, the two sat together, each grateful for the other. She began to feel better, but could not shake the feeling of the trouble that lay ahead.

7 - EXPLORATION

Shortage would best describe the situation in Epoch. Between the growing population, and the expansion of several businesses to produce goods from the anticipated refinery, there was a significant strain on already exhausted resources. Chronic shortages continued in labor and materials such as ores, lumber, and refined products like paper and glass. Critical items from the warehouse, such as copper wire, were being depleted to critical levels.

Jake and the other council members had authorized overtime for all the publicly-run projects, including construction of the refinery. Most working-age people in Epoch were getting used to working fifty hours or more each week.

Even with all the work, the last few months were among the best that Alec and Jordan had ever experienced. They worked the expected long hours at the Re-Discovery Center, but their priority, as dictated by Jake and the commander, remained to practice flying in preparation for the longer flights needed for reconnaissance work. Skipping reserve rotation was one of the benefits, and even Jake was easier on Alec, permitting him to occasionally avoid church attendance.

Their celebrity status had not worn off, and many of their friends requested airplane rides or stories about their flights and what they had seen. Their flight time was limited since the Re-Discovery Center could only spare enough fuel for one tank per week, with the rest going to teams working on proto-type vehicles. When not flying or working, both spent their time plotting new areas to explore and inspecting various aircraft components for wear or improvements.

By the end of the fall season, they had explored a fifty-mile radius around Epoch, discovering the ruins of old towns and roads taken back by nature. From what they did find, there was not too much left. Unless the exterior walls had been made from brick, they were crumbled to nothing or had caved in. Most of those made from brick had collapsed roofs. They took pictures of places that looked promising, but all were in poor condition and unlikely to contain much useable material.

A longer flight north to the town that Jake had originally pointed out showed the most promise. It had been nicknamed "Coppertown," in the hope that there would be a great deal of copper to be salvaged there. An attempt had been made to mine copper near Epoch, but even a small amount required too much work to mine and get to a useable state. Sending a salvage team to Coppertown would be a faster means, and there was the bonus of other re-useable items they expected to find.

However, it was discovered on approach to the town that the one major bridge along the road had collapsed. Building a new bridge with limited labor and materials was a useless option and hope turned towards a slightly longer, alternate route that would prove to be advantageous. If an alternate road turned out to be impractical, then Coppertown would have to wait, and another destination would have to be found.

Alec and Allison had agreed to examine this new route and assess what it would take to clear and rebuild the highway that led to it from Epoch. The route had no major bridges but had been rejected initially because it crossed over a major dam. After a few hundred years, both Jake and the commander had ruled out the route as both thought that the dam would already have collapsed. Now, they could only hope that the dam was still there and stable enough to carry traffic for a few months while they salvaged materials from the abandoned town.

"I can barely make out where the highway was," Allison said as she peered out of a side window. "There are so many trees down there." Although Alec was flying the plane as slowly as he dared, they were still moving too fast for a good look. They made several passes over sections so that Allison could view landscape details for the rough map she was drawing.

"What's your Dad's plan for this highway, anyway?" she asked. "It'll take years for us to rebuild it entirely."

Alec shifted his position at the controls. “He expects that the highway will be grown over with trees and vegetation, but if there aren’t big washouts or landslides, and if the dam is still standing, the plan is to take one of the big bulldozers up here when the refinery comes online. It wouldn’t take too long to make a rough road where the highway used to be. We wouldn’t be paving it, just filling it in with gravel. But if the road over the dam can’t be used, then building a new bridge over the river, or even taking a different path, would take years. Hey, are you okay with your map, or do we need to do one more pass?”

“No, I’m all good. We should be getting pretty close to the dam—I see the river off to the right, and I think I see a lake up ahead, which is a good sign that the dam is still there."

Alec squeezed her hand and then banked the plane in the direction of the lake. He loved flying so much, especially on days like this where the weather was calm and sunny. There were only a few small clouds in the sky and the sun beamed through the windshield giving the cockpit a warm and cozy feeling. He loved having Allison with him. They had become close, and he was beginning to contemplate asking her to marry him. He felt almost certain she would say yes, but he didn’t know if he was ready for the commitment.

Allison’s deductions had been correct, and soon the dam was in view. On their first fly-by, they could see the big concrete-and-earth structure still retaining the water from the lake, which, surprisingly, did not seem too silted as the spillways were still releasing water into the river below.

“It seems like there must’ve been some floods over the top of the dam not too long ago—look at those logs sitting on top of it,” said Alec. He pointed in front of them towards the dam.

“Oh, yeah, I see them, and there’s hardly any vegetation on top. Must’ve been a pile of water to clean it off like that. You can also see where the lake level used to be on the shorelines. Let’s do one more pass, and I’ll try to take a few more pictures so your dad can see for himself."

"Good idea," Alec said as he banked the plane again. "The city is only a couple of miles away, so once you have your pictures, we'll do a quick trip over it and then home. These passes have used up a bunch of fuel."

As they flew over Coppertown, they could make out where the streets and buildings had been, although very few buildings were left standing. Trees and other plants grew everywhere, and they even spotted a herd of deer grazing in what looked like the center of the city. Nearly all the houses in the suburbs had collapsed, and remains of vehicles that had been left on the streets could be vaguely identified.

"Wow, this is amazing!" Alec said, "Left unattended, you'd never even be able to tell that this city even existed in another few hundred years."

"Yeah, do you think that there's anything else salvageable down there? I can't imagine that there'd be too much."

"The copper will definitely be good. There'll be oxidization on the outside of the wires and pipes, but it'll be salvageable. Other than that, I'm not sure—anything made of plastic, if it was out of the sun, and glass—that stuff lasts for thousands of years. There may also be things that have been stored that we can use."

As they came to the edge of the city, he turned the plan around and headed back. Allison took more pictures and worked on finishing her map.

He wished they didn't have to return so soon and had hoped they would have enough fuel to fly the extra fifty miles north to the coordinates he had heard repeated through the shortwave radio. The few flights that had been made to Coppertown was the closest they had gotten so far, and it would take a week or two to produce another batch of fuel.

It was a short flight back to Epoch, and when they got there, he carried out one of his best landings. He steered the plane to the dock, and after securing it, they went to the town hall to see his father who was eager for news.

Jake ushered them into his office. "How was the flight, Alec?"

"Smooth—and I had a great co-pilot. The highway looks good, and the dam is still standing. Considering the age, we didn't see any significant issues—right Allison?"

"Nothing at all," she said. "There were a few miles of overgrowth where the highway had cut through a forest, but most of the road had only light vegetation on it. The dam is in good shape, and I took some pictures of it that I'll get developed for you at the Re-Discovery Center."

"Great," Jake said. "I'll talk with the council this week about getting people freed up for the salvage team. We already have a few working on replacing bulldozer and truck parts that didn't age well. The refinery should be at least partially online within a few weeks." He drummed his fingers impatiently on his desk then pointed a forefinger at Alec. "I almost forgot—could you take a mechanic and some parts up to the coal mine now? They're having problems with the conveyor belt, and I guess everything is at a standstill. If we ship parts up there by boat, they won't get there until tomorrow."

Alec shook his head. "Not sure if I'd have enough gas for that, Dad. We used most of the tank."

"Well, I happen to have an early Christmas present for you," his father said, grinning. "They've done a few trial runs at the new factory and happen to have about a hundred gallons of fuel that they don't know what to do with."

With another opportunity to fly his plane, Alec immediately agreed to go. "Sure, I'll leave as soon as I gas up. Send the mechanic down in about half an hour." His head was already in the air as he kissed Allison hastily and said he would see her later that afternoon.

On his way back to the dock, Alec ran across a small gathering of people listening to someone who sounded familiar. As he approached the group, he recognized Clyde as the speaker.

"Please—won't you reconsider?" Clyde asked the group as they began to leave.

Alec moved closer. "What are you up to, Clyde?"

"Trying to stop the stupid idea of rebuilding that road up to Coppertown,"

"Why would you do try to do that, and how are you going to stop it?" Alec felt annoyed with himself for starting the conversation.

"Your dad said that if I could get even a hundred signatures on this petition, he'd consider putting it up for a vote."

"That's because he knew you wouldn't get a hundred names. How many do you have so far?"

"Only five, and I've been at it for a week." Clyde sounded discouraged. He held up his clipboard and looked at the few names scrawled across the petition form. "I didn't think it would be this hard, but people have been so brainwashed about growth being such a good thing that they can't see the other side."

"But growth *is* good. It leads to better jobs and more of the things that we've been without since the Great Loss," Alec said. "Without growth, we'd stay like this forever—who wants that?"

Clyde became more animated and his voice hard-edged. "What we have already is more than we need. Growth *must* stop sometime. The planet is only so big; so why not stop now, instead of waiting until it's over-populated like before the Great Loss."

"There are only 10,000 people here in Epoch," Alec said, feeling annoyed. "It'll take a very long time for us to get to stage where we have to worry about overloading the planet. And even if we do get to that stage, we'll have invented new things that will compensate."

Clyde groaned. "Not as long as you think. The planet has barely begun to recover from the strains we put on it before the Loss." He waved the clipboard in the air. "I guess this is a waste of time. There are a few people who seemed a bit interested, but they couldn't be convinced that there's a different way to live. One where there's a status quo and not an unyielding drive for growth."

"This is the way it's always been," Alec said. "Growth means prosperity."

Clyde looked at him as though seeing something for the first time. "Is that what you think?" he asked incredulously. "Haven't you read any history? It has *not* always been this way." After a slight pause, he raised an arm in a sweeping motion towards the town. "I give up—this is a lost cause."

"Whatever—we're doing just fine, and we don't need what you're selling," Alec said. "I've got to get going. Unlike you, I need to work." At that moment, he wanted to put as much distance as possible between Clyde and himself and didn't wait to exchange any more words. He walked away wanting to get to the dock as quickly as he could.

As they taxied out into the open water, the mechanic looked visibly leery at the idea of flying, but Alec assured him it was safe. "We've made several flights already with no problems, and there are tons of failsafe mechanisms in this plane. We'll be there in about fifteen minutes." He moved to full throttle and started to skim across the lake for takeoff.

The lake by the coal mine was much smaller than Skater Lake. Both Jordan and Alec had practiced both takeoff and landing several times on the much shorter surface. The exercises had been worthwhile, and the flight and landing were quick and uneventful. Alec left the mechanic at the coal mine and was soon in the air again.

With almost a full tank of fuel and a sunny, cloud-free day, he could not resist the temptation to fly to the radio coordinates. He knew that Jordan should be along for this trip, but realized that if he returned to Epoch to get him, he would run into objections from his father and the commander about flight lengths and fuel wastage. But if he went there now, at least he would have enough fuel to look around for an hour. He banked the plane north. *Better to ask for forgiveness than permission.* He was nearly halfway to his destination before transmitting his plans to Epoch and shutting off the radio before hearing the reply.

Within a half hour, he was flying over Coppertown, and he noticed what might have been a sizable university grounds on the outskirts. The brick buildings were still standing, and he hoped there would be some valuable salvage material and equipment from the labs and libraries inside. He continued to travel north, and soon he crested over a series of high hills close to his target coordinates.

He was unsure of what would be there, but all that he saw was the same scenery as that on the way to the site: trees, hills, and water. He brought the plane as low as he dared and began to circle over the valley.

On the fourth pass, he noticed it. In the water of a small lake deep in the valley, there was something that did not look natural. He flew over in a final pass, this time verifying the shape of a structure at the bottom of the lake. There were no clear features, but he could see the straight lines of a single building and its surface was very white.

His elation was short-lived, however, as the engine on the small plane began to sputter, followed by clouds of smoke coming out of the cowling. The lake below was too small to land on, so he urged the struggling plane higher to get over the ridge of hills in front of him. He managed to gain enough altitude then turned the engine off before the smoke obliterated everything he could still see.

A large lake stretched out in front of him. The plane descended quickly, and with his hand clenched on the yoke, he tried to maintain the altitude as he neared the lake. The plane glided over the water, clipping only a few trees on the lake's edge. The plane resisted being properly positioned for the water landing, and the touchdown was hard as the floats dug into the water. It soon came to a stop, and he breathed a heavy sigh of relief and sat back in his seat.

He looked at his surroundings and noticed that he had landed at the end of the lake, which fed into a small river. The water moved slowly towards the river, and the plane floated along with it. He tried the radio, but within steep valley walls, it was of no use, and he kicked himself for not sending in a distress call while still in the air. The plane continued to drift towards the river, and he knew that the lake narrowed and that there were large boulders near the river's entrance. He judged the distance to the shore at some fifty feet, so he grabbed a rope from the cargo area and got out of the plane.

Standing on a pontoon, he fastened the rope to the plane, and then hanging on to the other end jumped into the lake and began to swim towards the shoreline. By the time he reached the shore, the rope was taut, and there was no way he could pull more without some kind of leverage. Still hanging onto the rope, he followed the drifting plane until he came upon an old tree, part of which had fallen into the lake. He wrapped the rope around it, and using another log for leverage, brought he plane towards the shore, managing to get one of the floats to rest against the fallen log.

With the plane secured, Alec dropped to the ground, exhausted both physically and mentally. He had no idea of what to do next. As he caught his breath, he decided that the first order of business was to inspect the plane. He lifted the engine flap and confirmed what he had been thinking. There was a large crack on one of the cylinder heads, like the problem encountered when they first tested the engine, but he thought it had been fixed. *What a place to break down. I must be at least 150 miles away from home.*

He checked the contents of the cargo hold and found a tool-kit and the emergency supplies his mother had insisted they take with them. There was food, minimal camping gear, and a medical kit. The sun was starting to set, and he found a flat, clear area near the lake and set up camp. He built a fire and ate some of the emergency rations, then sat back and tried to figure out a plan to get back home. His bigger problem was one of direction. From the air, he knew which way to go, but on the ground everything looked different. He could estimate the general direction, but could easily miss Epoch by thirty or forty miles on foot. He finally decided he would take the magnetic compass out of the plane in the morning. With the old maps that were in the plane, he would be able to follow a direct route towards Epoch.

In the morning, he restarted the fire, made soup from the provisions in the emergency kit, removed the compass from the plane, and planned his route. There was enough food for a week if he was careful with it, and walking the 150 miles would likely take ten days if he kept a good pace. This gave him a degree of confidence that he had a workable plan to get home.

After breakfast, he picked up the emergency pack and started in the most promising direction. He had little experience in the wilderness and was amazed by the amount of wildlife that surrounded him. His only weapon was a knife, and he tried not to think of what would happen if he ran into a bear or wolf. After a few miles, he noticed a raven that seemed to be following him and watching intently.

That may explain the feeling I've been having. The same feeling in the tram with the dog on the side of the road. He quickened his pace and tried not to think about it.

By mid-afternoon, he had made better progress than expected, and as he reached the top of a hill, he could see that the path, at least for today, was flat. He looked up and was momentarily distracted by the sight of the raven, causing him to trip over an exposed root and tumble some forty feet down the steep hill. Aside from the cuts and gashes to his body, he felt a searing pain in his right ankle.

He laid back and put his head on the ground. A short time later, he awoke after drifting in and out of consciousness. The sun was beginning to set. His ankle still throbbed, but he sat up with some effort. He knew that he was weak and had lost a considerable amount of blood. His medical kit was still with him, and he bandaged the worst of his cuts.

Searching for painkillers, he was puzzled to see a roll of paper he didn't recall packing tied with string at the bottom of the kit. He untied the string, and despite his predicament, began to laugh out loud as two marijuana joints rolled into his hand. He read the note. "Use as needed when you want to fly a little higher."

Clyde! He must've put done this the day he asked to look inside the plane it?

He examined the two joints. *Why not?*

Having never smoked before, he was unaccustomed to the smoke and began to cough after his first puff, but he kept trying and by the time the joint had burned up, he no longer felt much pain. The experience was not at all what he had imagined. He found that his thinking was clearer and quicker, and with his pain temporarily suppressed, he could gather some nearby sticks and start a fire.

As the fire grew, he propped himself up against a nearby log and reflected on all the new sensations that he was experiencing. Then he felt that he was being watched again and looked up into a nearby tree directly at the raven. He was more acutely aware of being watched now, and could sense the location of the raven.

Within an hour, these sensations began to dissipate and were steadily replaced by waves of depression. He thought about the dangerous position he was now in, how much longer it would take to get home now, and the more pressing issue of having to gather food. His head buzzed as he drifted into an uncomfortable sleep under the watchful eye of the raven.

8 - RESCUE

Robert was having a very productive afternoon in his laboratory. He was nearing a breakthrough in the development of a cement-and-lead mixture that would encase the radioactive leak found some years before. In the hallway outside the lab, the sound of running grew closer, and without warning, the door burst open. Lauren ran across the room to her father.

"Dad, come outside! They found an injured man in the forest!" she said. She was out of breath and noticeably distraught.

"Who?" he asked, startled by the intrusion and his daughter's appearance.

She struggled to catch her breath. "It's a stranger. A hunting team found him near Bear Lake."

They went outside and saw a crowd of people that were following the men carrying an improvised stretcher with the stranger. Robert pushed his way through the crowd and looked at the unconscious man. He looked young and was not very big. His wounds were serious, and Robert directed the men carrying the stretcher to take him to the nursing station that was just down the hall from the Research Lab.

Once there, Lauren and a few others spent several hours tending to the stranger and left him in a quiet sleep. "He was pretty beat up," Lauren said to her dad as she returned to the Research Lab. I think his ankle is sprained or fractured as well, but he will be ok."

As she spoke, they both heard noises coming from the nursing station. When they entered the room, they saw that the stranger was now awake.

Alec saw a tall young woman and a giant-sized man enter the room he was in. "Who are you, and where am I?" he demanded.

“Full of questions—you must be feeling better," Robert said. You must’ve been in a big accident to end up as wounded as you did."

“Plane crash," Alec said, confirming Robert’s fears.

“Really! I’ve only read about those things," Robert replied.

“I was checking out some kind of structure in the lake when I started to have engine trouble."

“There’s a structure in the lake?” Robert said in surprise.

“Yeah, there is something in the lake I was flying over. Back in my town, we hear a set of coordinates on the shortwave radio a couple of times a day. That’s why I’m up here—to see what’s at that location.”

Robert could hardly believe what Alec was telling him. “We’ve heard them as well—on our radio starting about twenty years ago. They point to Little Bear Lake. Several teams have tried to find something there but never could. But then if it was in the lake, that would explain why they never found anything.”

“Where am I?” Alec asked.

“My name is Robert, and this is my daughter Lauren. You are in a village called Percipience.”

“My name is Alec and my town is called Epoch.”

“I can get a radio message over to Epoch if you have a frequency that I can use." Robert said.

Alec gave Robert the main frequency that Epoch used and then drifted back to sleep.

With that, Robert left Lauren to watch over their patient and went to meet with the elders to explain what had happened and to ask for their opinion on what should be done next. His own idea was to make radio contact with Epoch and let them know that Alec was in their care.

"You're right," said an elder at the assembly, "it would have been better if the boy had died. But he didn't, and regardless of what we think about Epoch, we should do the right thing and let his parents know." His proposal was met with unanimous agreement.

They were more interested in Robert's story about the structure that Alec had described seeing in the lake and agreed to send a small team to investigate. When the group dispersed, Robert made his way to the town center to use the radio equipment. *Maybe we can use this opportunity to find out more about Epoch from this boy.*

"Epoch, please come in, Epoch, please come in." Robert said leaning into the radio microphone. After a few seconds, a reply came through.

"This is Epoch, who is this?" The voice sounded anxious.

Robert took in a deep breath. "This is Percipience, a village a few hundred miles from your location. I'm contacting you to let you know that we have Alec here. He's been badly hurt in a plane crash, but he seems to be doing well."

"What?" the voice squawked. "Please hold on." After a short silence, the radio crackled with renewed intensity. "This is Jake, Alec's father—is my son all right? Where is he, and who are you?"

Robert explained Alec's injuries in detail and gave the location of Percipience. "Alec gave me this radio frequency so that I could contact you to let you know he's all right."

"Thank God," Jake said. "We were so worried and had feared the worst. Two hundred miles—that's quite a distance. It'll take two or three weeks to get there by horseback."

"Oh!" Robert said with feigned surprise. "You don't have another plane that you could send up for him?" He knew that Epoch's first and only aircraft was the one that had crashed.

"No, we do not," Jake said. He paused to think of a good reason to give on why Epoch owned no other planes. Offering too much information to someone he knew nothing about was not his intention.

Robert broke the silence. "Okay, it'll probably be at least six to eight weeks before Alec is ready for any kind of journey. May I suggest that we take care of him, and we can discuss how he gets back home a bit later? I'll get him to this radio as soon as possible so that he can talk to you himself. Probably by tomorrow."

"I can't tell you how thankful we are for all of your help," Jake said. He sounded relieved and grateful. "Yes, that sounds like a good idea. Please tell him that we love him and that we're praying for him."

"Our radio doesn't broadcast for too long at a time before needing a recharge," Robert said, "but we'll talk to you again tomorrow at about the same time and give you an update."

"Thanks, yes, of course, talk to you tomorrow," Jake replied.

Robert flipped the power switch on the radio. *Well, it's now begun.* He hoped that he was wrong about how it would all turn out, but felt sure that bad things lay ahead.

Lauren and her helpers tended to Alec's wounds and spoon fed him soup before he drifted back to sleep. When she returned to her hut, her father was waiting for her.

"Lauren, we need to talk," he said. He led her to the fire ring next to the hut. There was no one there, and they sat on a log near the extinguished fire. "I'm going to ask you to do something for me, and I don't want you to question as to why or to try to figure it out."

She was surprised by his words and had never seen him as serious. Nor had he ever made a request of anything like this before.

"We need to get Alec well quickly, and then get him back to his own village," he said. "While he's here, I don't want him to see any of our advanced technology, especially the work we're doing in the Research Center. I don't want him to see or hear about your abilities, and don't mention anything about the nuclear-weapons storage facility we found. I want him to have as little contact as possible with anyone else. I'll tell the elders of the other huts to instruct their own not to avoid him, but to not encourage conversation either."

Lauren's jaw dropped as she listened. This was so unlike her father, and questions ran through her mind, but he had said she couldn't ask about anything. Then she remembered the plan he had mentioned after she had seen the plane during The Games.

"I think that Alec is a good person," Robert said, "but he must return to his own home as soon as he's able. Also, when you're with him, I want you to find out as much as possible about Epoch. Things like the number of people there and types of technology. Maybe you can get him to show you the location of their mines and other remote centers as well."

"I guess . . ." she said. "I don't see the harm in his knowing more about us, but I'll do it." She felt perplexed by her father's request as she followed him back to the hut.

9 - PREPARATION

News about Alec and Percipience spread like wildfire through Epoch. Though missing only a few days, many had feared the worst, and the news that he was alive was a renewed celebration for the town. No one was happier than Allison, who had spent the time in her room crying and regretting that she had not gone with him.

"Allison, don't be ridiculous—we're not leaving right now to travel on horseback through a few hundred miles of unknown wilderness and mountains and at least two canyons to get him," Jordan pleaded. He and Kimberly were in Allison's room and watching as she frantically packed the necessities she would need for the trip.

"He's right," Kimberly said. "Let's wait a day or two. The man where Alec is now said he'd get him to radio us by tomorrow." The thought of hearing Alec's voice seemed to calm her, and she paused in her frenzied arrangements.

"So all we know is that the plane came down, that he's hurt, and that the people there are taking care of him?" she said. "What's the name of the town?"

"Percipience," Kimberly replied. "And, yeah, that's all we know right now. I'm still surprised that another town is so close to us, and we didn't even know about it."

"Me too!" Jordan said. "They have a radio, which makes it really strange that they didn't hear us before or that we didn't hear them since we monitor for new communications so often."

Allison added more clothes in her backpack.

"What are you doing? You're not still thinking of making the trip, are you?" Kimberly asked.

"No, not now anyway, but I can't miss his call, so I'm going to move into the town hall. I want to be right beside the radio."

Kimberly and Jordan looked at each other and shook their heads and laughed. They helped her finish packing and accompanied her to the radio room.

Jake and Claire were equally happy to find out that their son was alive. They had sent searchers to the nearest ridge to see if a signal could be picked up from the plane's radio, but all efforts left them feeling helpless. Even Alec's dog, Koda, was less dispirited and restless than he had been since it was first learned that Alec was missing.

Jake, however, did not accept the radio recharge account that Robert had given him. He also shared Jordan's concern as to why they had never heard from Percipience. *It's almost like they've been hiding from us—but for what reason? If they can build a radio, they could easily build a battery system to keep it going.* He wondered about the size of the town and how advanced they could be. If he could believe what Robert had told him, the distance was too far to travel without serious planning. And it would take two to three weeks on horseback, given the mountains and other terrain to be covered. *Alec must find out as much as he can while he's up there without saying much about us. There'll be people around him when he's at their radio—it won't be easy to tell him.*

One positive point was the northerly location of Percipience. This would offer a perfect reason to clean up the road leading to Coppertown that Alec and Allison had scouted. Percipience could not be more than fifty or seventy-five miles north of there, and with the prospect of new markets and labor, convincing the elected officials to accelerate the road construction would be easy. There was even the prospect of setting up a new satellite village next to Percipience instead of to the south as had been originally planned.

Of course, he would have to deal with the commander. With gasoline engines and the associated fuel becoming a reality, the commander had been pushing for military trucks and other equipment to be built first. With an advanced village being so close, Jake knew that the commander would now push harder to ensure the security of Epoch. He had agreed that Epoch needed both defensive and offensive strength but believed the commander was power hungry. With sufficient resources under his command, he could easily attempt a coup on the government, and hence, Jake's office. The obvious solution was to replace the commander with someone loyal, and that is exactly what Jake planned to do.

He felt confident and in control of all that needed to be done and headed to his office to set his plans into motion.

As he passed the warehouse, he saw a sign on a street vendor's stall that made him pause. He read the large, green print. "Grow Your Own!"

He approached the stall and was unsurprised to see Clyde sitting behind the stand. A variety of small starter plants, books, and seed packages were on display.

"Clyde! What are you doing? I'm going to call the commander and have you arrested!"

"For what?" He picked up the book that had slipped from his hands. "Selling tomato plants and seeds?"

Jake looked down at the stand and realized the plants were all vegetables, mostly tomatoes. He shifted his feet. "Well, what's this all about?"

Clyde smiled and sat down again. "Instead of raising cattle for beef and the greenhouse hydroponic crap, then locking it away and making people pay for it, I'm offering an alternative. Grow your own, good-tasting food. And all from heirloom seed, too. Want to try some?" He held out a plate with tomato pieces spread out for tasting.

Jake swiped the plate aside, knocking the fruit to the ground. "Look, I know you're up to something here—selling pot perhaps?"

"Not a green leaf here, sir," Clyde said, still smiling.

"What are these?" Jake pointed to two clipboards.

"One is for pre-orders for, uh, plants that I don't have here. The other is a waste of time. It's the petition we talked about to get that stupid highway stopped."

Sensing defeat in Clyde's voice, Jake asked, "How's that coming along?"

"You already know the answer. Pretty much the whole town is for re-building the highway, and that was before the news about Percipience. Now, everyone wants to be connected to it."

Jake smiled. "You're right—I did know, but I had to let you discover it for yourself. Look, I think you're a pretty smart kid and probably understand better than most how things work. You must realize by now that there's no way you can win this planet-friendly campaign of yours."

"I'm not giving up yet. I'll find a way to get people to understand."

Jake sighed loudly. "I could let you learn another lesson on your own here. But I'll try to tell you now instead. Look, not only is the deck stacked completely against you, you don't even get a card to play. Thousands of years of history have proven there's no way to stop growth." He turned on his heels, feeling a sense of victory, and continued on his way.

Clyde watched Jake walk away and realized that despite his bureaucratic attitude, what he had said was true.

****

Jake had stayed away from his office during most of the time since Alec's disappearance. He opened the door and was greeted by a tall pile of neglected paperwork needing his attention. He fired off several memos requesting meetings to discuss his plans and continued to work on the most urgent items. After a while, he looked out through his window and saw that the street lights were on and realized it was very late.

He turned off his desk lamp and put on his coat. Before leaving, he opened a cabinet drawer, reached into a bag, and dug out a tablet that he placed in his coat pocket. The office was empty by now, but he looked around nonetheless to make certain no one saw him. He locked the drawer and left.

On his way home, he stopped at the base of the water tower and unlocked the door to the room beneath it. It was not until he had entered the dark room and closed the door that he flipped on the light switch. He made his way through a maze of pumps, tanks, and pipes to a series of tanks that injected various chemicals into the water. This guaranteed its safety so that it could be stored without any unwanted algae growth. He lifted the lid of a tank, removed the tablet from his coat pocket, and dropped it into the water. He watched it slowly sink to the bottom where it rested close to its almost-dissolved predecessor.

He nodded approvingly, closed the lid, and left the room.

10 - HEALING

Alec awoke and could see the first rays of sun coming through the window. He tested his limbs, and aside from his splinted leg, everything seemed to be getting better. A small boy came into the room. “Hi,” he said, as he walked towards Alec’s bed.

“Hello, my name is Alec, what’s yours?"

“Chris. They said you flew here. How did you do that?"

“I built a plane…” Alec said. The door opened, and he raised his head to see over the boy’s head.

“Good morning, Alec,” Robert said, entering hesitantly at first. “Chris, would you mind running along?” The boy looked at Alec one last time and bolted out of the room.

“How are you feeling today?”

“Better," Alec replied, his voice still thick. “How long was I out? It feels like I slept for a week.”

“Actually, only one night. We found you two days ago, and you arrived at our village yesterday. You’ve lost a lot of blood, and some of your wounds are deep. It also appears that you fractured your ankle. All in all, you were pretty banged up." Robert proceeded to check Alec’s temperature and other vital signs. “Good. The fever is going down and the infection is under control.” He paused and looked at Alec who had raised himself to a sitting position. “I contacted your dad yesterday via radio,” he said. “He knows you’re all right, and I told him that you’d probably talk with him today."

"Yes! I need to talk him," Alec said. He suddenly felt stronger. "How long before I can get moving? I'm sorry—what was your name again?"

"Robert, and I don't think you'll be moving around much for the next few days. Then limited movement for a week or so then crutches for several weeks. After you have some breakfast, we'll let you have a quick chat with your parents, and then take it from there."

Alec was surprised at how hungry he felt, and he quickly finished the soup that Robert had brought. He noticed that half the items in the soup were unrecognizable to him, but it was delicious, and he felt much better. In addition to the food, Robert also had brought a cup of warm, dark liquid with a unique taste that Alec liked.

"Coffee," Robert said before Alec could ask. "We make it from a combination of dandelion and ginseng roots, and I have at least one cup each morning before doing anything."

The door opened again, and Lauren entered. "How is my patient doing today?" she asked brightly.

"Your patient? Isn't there a doctor here?" Alec asked in an anxious tone.

"We had a few people look in on you," Robert said, "but everyone here pretty much trusts Lauren's instincts."

"Hmm . . . maybe we should amputate that leg after all," she said playfully.

Robert asked Lauren for help with the radio, and they left Alec alone. When they were out of earshot, Robert reminded her of their conversation the day before.

"You can talk as much as you want about our culture and food, but the machine shop, Research Center, and the nuclear weapon site that we found are off limits."

.

Although still perplexed by her father's concerns, she assured him that she would be careful of what she said.

Robert had a few technicians modify a base radio so that it operated just like the portable ones, shutting down after a few minutes of use. He and Lauren brought in this radio and showed Alec how to operate it, explaining that only a few minutes of transmitter time would be permitted before the unit shut off to recharge. He keyed the transmitter, and within a few seconds of trying to reach Epoch, he heard Allison's voice.

"Alec, how are you? I've been so worried about you and missed you so much!" Allison's voice gushed through the radio.

Clearly embarrassed, he said that he was doing fine and that Dr. Lauren was taking very good care of him.

"Dr. Lauren?" Allison asked.

"Yes, she's the best doctor here. I guess she must use her intelligence to make up for her looks. She has a large wart on her nose and isn't too easy on the eyes." Alec said, looking directly at Lauren. Lauren responded by pushing gently on his injured leg, causing him to flinch.

He was aware that time was at a premium, and he finished his conversation by assuring Allison that he was fine, but it would be several weeks before he was ready to return to Epoch. He explained that they could speak only for few minutes, and they agreed on set times. Then the red light on the radio appeared, cutting off their communications.

"That girl sounded like she cares a lot for you," Lauren said after the radio went silent.

"She's a close friend," Alec said. His unexpected answer surprised him.

"A wart? Really? You could've come up with something more creative. How about chiseled teeth or a unibrow?"

“It was the first thing that popped into my head."

Robert interrupted their teasing banter. "While you’re stuck in that bed for the next few days, we’ll leave the radio where you can reach it. That way, you won't have us listening to your conversations. In the meantime, rest up, and if you need anything at all, just let Lauren or me know."

Alec wanted to talk more but felt overcome by exhaustion. With a full stomach and the energy expended in conversation, he fell asleep before he could thank them for their help.

Later that day, he was again communicating with Allison before his father interjected. "So glad to hear your voice, Alec. We were terribly worried about you."

"Good to hear you too, Dad. Tell Mom and Koda that I said hi and look forward to talking with Mom soon. The people here are treating me well, and they’ve even moved a radio into my room."

Jake saw his opportunity and jumped on it. "Are they there now?"

"No, Lauren left about a half hour ago."

"Okay," Jake replied. "Alec, I’m only going to say this only once. Please find out as much as you can about their village and keep me updated. And there’s no need to tell them a lot about us, understand?"

He thought about what his father had said "Yes, I’ve got it, I’ll keep you updated as best as I can. Tell Jordan that there’s a new lake at those mystery coordinates and that there’s a structure in the lake."

The red light on the transmitter came on again, ending their chat before he could elaborate on his discovery. He thought more about his father’s words and knew that he would be cautious about a new town so close to them that had stayed hidden for hundreds of years. He had wondered the same thing himself and intended to get some answers when he could move around again.

Robert sat on a stool in his lab, the portable radio that he had used to listen to Alec's conversation standing on the table next to him. He sighed, realizing he had been right to feel nervous about contact with Epoch. He sighed as he concluded he would have to proceed with the plans that he and the elders had discussed.

The next morning, Robert told Lauren that he and a few of the elders were going to head back up to the nuclear-weapons site. They would get a small sample of radioactive material so that he could test his new cement.

"Isn't that dangerous?" she asked.

"Not really, we still have those radiation suits that we used a few years ago, and I have a container that will keep the sample safe. We should only be gone a few days. In the meantime, you're in charge of making sure that our new resident is taken care of so that he heals quickly. We're also going to send a few people up to Little Bear Lake to see about the structure that Alec said he saw in the lake."

Lauren felt torn by this news. She wanted to make the trip to the lake but knew that she was needed in Percipience.

For the next few days, Alec talked to Epoch frequently each day from his bed and spent a great deal of time talking with Lauren. On the third day, she came in pushing what appeared to be a brand-new wheelchair. "Time to get out of that bed," she said.

"You're that doctor with a wart on her nose," he replied. With some difficulty, they managed to get him into the wheelchair, and soon they were moving out of the nursing station and into the village.

Alec remembered nothing of his arrival into Percipience, so everything was new to him. The first thing he noticed was the dearth of people compared to Epoch.

"It's still early," Lauren said when he asked her about it. "People try to get most of their chores done in the morning, so they have more time for other things. It'll get busier after lunch when people return from the fields and gathering food. Did you want to see our greenhouse?"

"Greenhouse? Sure, that sounds like fun. We have one at Epoch, too."

As Lauren pushed the wheelchair down the dirt path in the direction of the greenhouse, he asked about the small buildings scattered among the trees.

"Those are the clan huts where we sleep and eat. There are usually six or seven families per hut. Here, let me show you. They kind of tie into the greenhouse anyhow." She turned off the main path and up a smaller one that led to one of the huts. The entry door was open, and she pushed him in ahead of her. She greeted the few people already there preparing lunch and introduced them to him.

He was shocked when he realized that families meant not just parents and children, but grandparents and even great grandparents. He could understand the combined large kitchen and eating room, but had a hard time understanding the common sleeping room. "Everyone sleeps in the same room?" He asked.

"Of course," Lauren replied, "How else would you do it?"

He explained that in Epoch, adults had their own bedrooms until they were married, and then they would share one room.

"Sounds kind of lonely and a big waste of building materials for a room that's only slept in. Your huts must be huge, though, to have thirty or so bedrooms."

He laughed. "That *would* be a big building. No, there are separate buildings for each family. Usually, just parents and their children live in one building."

Lauren seemed amazed and was unable to fathom not being with her grandparents and cousins every day or the amount of materials needed to build so many dwellings.

She decided not to pursue the topic and showed him the rest of the hut: electric appliances, sinks, and the large washrooms and shower areas. She told him how the water from the sinks and showers is piped through a filtration unit then up into a water tower for later use in the greenhouse.

"Why go through all of the bother of conserving water? There are massive amounts of it flowing all around us."

"The main reason is because we can't put water back into the river as clean as we take it out. Even with good filtration, it still has extra pollutants and oils in it. But it's clean enough for our plants."

It was his turn to not understand, but he had no opportunity to ask more questions as she wheeled him out of the hut and back onto the route to the greenhouse.

He pointed to some chairs that were suspended in the air by a large cable. "What are they?"

"That's our transportation system," she said. "We call it the Air-Chair. It's a network of chairlifts running between key points in Percipience. We use it during harvest season to move crops from one clan hut to the other, and the elderly use it to get wherever they need to go."

"The chairs aren't moving now," he said. "How often does it run?"

"We don't have enough excess power to run it all the time, so usually it goes for a few hours in the afternoon and hardly at all in the winter time. If we time things right, we can take it back from the greenhouse when we're done there."

When they arrived at the greenhouse, Lauren showed Alec the rows of vegetables at various stages of maturity, medicinal plants such as ginger, garlic, and trees including fruit and a Eucommia. As they went through, she carefully maneuvered the wheelchair so that Alec did not see the bug farm and synthetic meat operations.

"Epoch's greenhouse is much bigger," Alec said, "with a picnic area in the middle. How many people can get food from here? How is it rationed out?"

"There's no rationing." she said. "During the summer, each hut is responsible for taking care of a large garden, and the crop is shared with the other huts. Some of the harvest is eaten right away, and what remains is stored for the winter in cold rooms under each hut. But this greenhouse produces enough greens and other things all through the winter."

"Someday it won't be big enough as your village expands."

She laughed and waved off his prediction. "Our village hasn't expanded in decades, and we have very strict rules on having children. Our elders determine the genetic pairing and after a woman is finished having children, she's given a pill that prevents her from having anymore."

"That's horrible! Controlling how many children you can have is one thing, but dictating who the father and mother should be is *so* wrong. What happens if a woman doesn't like the man chosen?"

She laughed again. "We don't have to do it the natural way, silly. I mean, we never know who the father is—it's all done artificially."

"But why is it done this way— it's all so unnatural."

"Because it's also necessary. Let me give you a little puzzle." They came to a seating area, and she sat down on a wooden bench, positioning the wheelchair so that they faced each other. "What if I gave you a box with five female and five male mice? Every day you'd open the box and clean it out, and then put in enough food for one hundred mice. At the end of six months, how many mice are in the box?"

"One hundred," he said confidently.

"That's right—population increase to match the food supply if there are no predators around. Look at us humans—we don't have any predators, and with our tools and knowledge, there's a great deal of food we can consume. If we were like mice, our population would grow into the billions. And that's not even the biggest problem. We wouldn't just be eating our food but nearly every other animal and plant's food too, and that would lead to the extinction of many species."

"But what about controlling the selection of the father and mother," he said.

"Okay, so with humans, if there's an abundance of food, and everyone has babies with whomever they please, the genetic paring will be random. There will be no dominant traits to cull out unwanted mutations. We need to be at least a bit selective about it to avoid the propagation of the mutations." She told him about The Games and how part of their purpose was to determine physical and mental characteristics of people which were a contributing factor to the elders' pairing decisions.

She wondered, remembering her father's instructions, whether she should be telling Alec any of this. But she had surely not revealed anything that would be harmful. "It's why people are starting to live longer here. Those who are healthier at older ages more often have their great-grandkids chosen for more children."

He felt dazed by all she had said, most of it going against all he had been taught. "I have to admit I'd never thought about any of it that way before," he said. "But it does explain what I've noticed today. Though I haven't seen too many people here yet, those that I have seen are much taller and stronger than the average person in Epoch. How do you know what population to grow to before you clamp it down?"

She considered what he had asked and shrugged her shoulders. "That's a tougher question, and no one has the right answer. Here in Percipience, two thousand was the number chosen, plenty for diversity in genes, thoughts, and skills, yet still manageable." But there's been lots of discussion over the last few years about expanding out to a new village a few hundred miles to the southwest, closer to the ocean."

"Yeah, we've had the same discussions in Epoch, but I haven't heard much more about it lately." Another question crossed his mind, and he asked it before thinking about whether he should "Do you know how many babies you're going to be allowed to have?"

She immediately changed the subject. "I think it's time for you to rest now. Let's see if we can still catch the Air Chair back to the town center."

The greenhouse was a key gathering point in Percipience, and there was an Air-Chair platform outside the entrance. They got themselves seated and strapped the wheelchair behind them. She pulled on the cable beside her as she explained how everything worked and was self-operated.

Their chair got picked up by the moving cable, and they started to move. He was struck by the simplicity and smoothness of the ride. "We're not too far from the ground," he said as the chair wound its way through the trees.

She looked out at the scenery they passed. "Over the flat ground, it's only about ten feet, in other areas it may get as high as fifteen feet or so. I think it was built that way both for safety and ease of maintenance."

They soon reached the town-center platform, and the chair disengaged from the main cable. By the time they arrived back to the nursing station, he was exhausted and fell immediately into a deep sleep. She watched for a while as he slept, then left and ran into her father outside. He was with a group of men carrying a large case.

"Dad! I wasn't expecting you back quite so soon."

"We made good time," her father said, hugging her. "And we have some good samples from the nuclear-weapons site." He pointed to the large case.

"Is it safe to have that here?" she asked.

"Completely." He demonstrated by taking off his radiation monitor and passing it around the box. An occasional beep could be heard from the unit but nothing that indicated dangerous amounts of radiation.

He instructed the men to bring the case into the Research Center. "How is your patient coming along?" he asked

"Really well. His wounds are healing, and today, I took him on a wheelchair tour of our greenhouse. We took the Air-Chair back."

"Good." he said. "The sooner he gets better, the sooner he can get back to his village."

"Why are you in such a rush to get rid of him, and why all of the secrecy? He seems like a really nice person."

"You'll have to trust me for a while longer, honey. I think you already may have uncovered part of the answer on your own." He looked at her, and she frowned bemusedly.

"Me? What answer?"

"A month ago, you mentioned that you were having visions of a pyramid while meditating," he said. "I think we have part of this puzzle of yours sorted out."

"What do you mean?"

"This morning, I got word back from the team that went up to Little Bear Lake. I didn't get all the details because of the short radio time, but they found something under the water there."

"In the lake?" she asked excitedly.

"Yes," he said, "They could only dive a short distance down, but it looks like the top of the structure is under about fifty feet of water, and it appears to be in the shape of a pyramid though they couldn't tell for sure."

She felt her heart begin to beat faster. "Did they say anything else?"

"No, that was all." he said. "But I remembered our conversation about your vision. Besides the pyramid, you said you got the feeling of great conflict and grief. You were right about the pyramid, and I think you're right about the conflict, too. I also think the source of that is Alec, and that's why he needs to get away from here as soon as possible."

Lauren's mind whirled. Her father was right. She did sense that there were great conflict and sadness associated with the pyramid. *But how could Alec be at the center of that?*

During the next few days, she took Alec on short tours of Percipience, showing him the various crops grown, and how they made clothes and paper from the hemp they grew.

"Why hemp?" he asked.

"It's far better than the usual alternatives." she said. "It grows quickly and is versatile. Did you know that an acre of hemp can produce as much paper as four acres of trees?"

"Hemp is illegal in Epoch," he said. "Other than it being a drug, I really don't know that much about it."

Cannabis and hemp are related, but they're different plants," she explained. "We grow both here, and I can't think of a reason why it would illegal."

He thought back to the night he smoked some after rolling down the hill and getting injured. "I'm not sure either, he said. "But it's been the law for a long time. I guess if it were legal, people would spend less money on liquor and other drugs. Maybe that's what started it. And by the way, I haven't seen any tractors or big machines here. Do you work all of the fields by hand?"

"Mostly," she replied. "We do have one tractor here that runs on wood gas, and we use that for tilling large fields. Other than that, it's all done by hand. It's not much work with a bunch of people on it all at once."

"And I've seen a lot of crops but no livestock. Do you get all your protein just from the vegetables?"

She answered without hesitation. "Mostly. We're not pure vegetarians, though. Each hut is given a yearly quota for fish and big game, but those numbers are low. I'm not sure how to describe this, but we also make a synthetic meat, which I don't think you've have tried yet. And we eat a fair number of bugs." She laughed when she saw his disgusted expression.

"Yuck! I could never do it."

"You've been doing that ever since you got here," she said, watching him turn pale. Don't worry; they're in nearly all the meals that we eat, though usually not in their natural form. Normally we grind them up." She couldn't help feeling amused seeing him recoil. "We grow them in crates in the greenhouse—they're easy to grow and very high in all sorts of nutrients."

He looked at her and wondered what he had eaten over the last few days. Everything had tasted fine, and he had enjoyed all his meals. He thought about his initial reaction and laughed.

"What's so funny? I thought you'd be mad at me for keeping this secret from you."

"I'd have done the same thing to you if the tables were turned. I was just laughing at the reaction most of the people in Epoch would have to eating bugs. How many other secrets are you keeping?"

"None, I swear," she said quickly and led them back towards to the town center.

He could tell a lie when he heard one and wondered what else she was keeping from him.

11 - MOBILIZATION

Jordan was the first to volunteer for the commander's team that would investigate the structure Alec had seen at Little Bear Lake. Altogether there would be twenty men heading up, and close to every horse in Epoch would be used to carry them and their tents, supplies, and explosives needed for the trip.

The commander was not in favor of the trip at first. He thought that any value in the structure would surely have been destroyed after being flooded with water. Jake, however, had a different opinion.

"commander, whoever put this campaign together—the shortwave broadcast and the covert building of the pyramid—were willing to go through a great deal of trouble and expense," Jake summarized during their meeting in his office. "I think there's a good chance that something of immense value is in there, and I sure don't want Percipience to have it. I'll make you a deal—get a squad up there quickly, make sure that it's well staffed so they can drain the lake, and see what this is all about. Do this and I'll promise you priority on building more of that military equipment you've been harassing me about."

The commander understood the give and take of politics and realized the message that Jake conveyed. Without sending a squad to investigate, he would never get his new equipment. And so he agreed, treating it like any other level of red tape to get through.

"Excellent," Jake said. "By the way, how's that proto-type truck working out? The Re-Discovery Center has promised to get me one in a few weeks."

The commander's mood brightened slightly. "The center did a great job on it. A few little things need changing, but I've been driving it for the last few days and am quite pleased. A dozen or so of these will make a big difference to our security. Actually, I need to head back to the DC now to show it off to some of the troops." The commander turned and headed towards the door.

"One more thing," Jake said as the commander reached for the door handle. "I want Jordan to lead this squad."

"Jordan? He's in the Reserves, and I have far more qualified people. I don't tell you how to manage Epoch, so please don't tell me how to manage operations in the DC." The commander felt his anger build. He'd had more than enough of this bureaucrat and could hardly wait for the day when Jake would answer to him.

"You have better qualified military personnel. I'll agree to that," Jake said, enjoying the commander's discomfort. "But this mission will be more about politics than military action. Percipience is close to this site, and I need someone who can think on his feet. I think Jordan has a natural ability." *And he will be loyal to me in case we find something there.*

The commander thought for a moment then reckoned that the sooner this was over, the sooner he would get his equipment. "Okay, you have a deal. Anything else?" he asked without checking his sarcasm.

"No, that is all, commander." Jake smiled back. His tone made it clear that the commander was dismissed.

At the time of this conversation, Robert was making his own plans. From the radio conversations he overheard between Alec and his father, Robert learned that a squad of people would be sent from Epoch to investigate the finding at Little Bear. Regardless if there might be anything of value in the flooded building or not, he and the elders agreed that Epoch should not get there first. They already had the advantage of technology and size; any further advantage would make them unstoppable.

To this end, Robert sent up a small group of men to Little Bear. They would have five weeks to drain the lake, based on the schedule that Jake had communicated to Alec before an Epoch contingent could get there. Robert's concern was the release of too much water at once. He instructed the team to use small, controlled explosions on the rocks that formed the lake's natural dam so that there would be no major flooding downstream. If all worked out as planned, they would have enough of the lake drained and at least a week to explore the pyramid.

He reviewed this plan with the elders at a campfire meeting. Good progress had been made on finding whatever might be at the bottom of Little Bear. "But what about the other plans—any progress there?" an elder asked.

Robert carefully considered his response. "I'm almost finished the calculations on what will be needed. I'll send them out to get the opinion of those of you who specialize in this area, but I don't think we can risk letting too many people know what we're up to."

"Good," the elder replied. "I agree—we must not let anyone outside this group in on what's going on."

"How about Lauren?" another elder asked. "I fear she's the wildcard. With her abilities, she may find out and then throw a wrench into our plans."

"Yes," Robert said. "I fear this as well, and I'm as careful around her as I can possibly be. Perhaps the distraction of taking care of the boy from Epoch will be enough to keep her occupied and off our trail for now."

"And if it doesn't?" the elder asked.

"Then I know what I need to do," he said gravely.

About a week later Alec told Robert about the team that Epoch was getting together to investigate the pyramid. "They are just getting things organized now. If they hold to their plan, they will be there in about five weeks."

"Hmm, that timing may work out very well with your recovery and return home. We could head out in a month or so to meet them and check your plane out at the same time. If the plane can be repaired, you could fly back, otherwise you could go back with that team."

Alec nodded, "That sounds pretty good, and it also lets us look at this structure which I have been dying to see."

With a plan to get back home in place, Alec was surprised by his lack of excitement. He had moved out of the nursing room into Lauren's Clan hut. Integrating quickly into the new expanded family structure, he looked forward to each day, especially the time spent with Lauren. Each morning, he was given chores by Lauren or her father. They usually involved food gathering or preparation exercise that would take the morning to complete. In the afternoon, he spent time with Lauren learning new skills, one of which was an introduction to meditation.

One midafternoon, he and Lauren sat on a rock atop Windmill Hill looking out over the valley. Comprising mostly of trees, the occasional field, and clan hut could be seen on sunny days. He looked at her as she sat in the lotus position, eyes closed, entirely at peace.

"You spend a lot of time at this. Does it get easier as you do it more often?" he asked.

"Of course," she replied. "After about five thousand sessions, you'll see that it's much easier." She giggled cheerily. "But really, after even a month, you'll find it not only easier but you'll start to see benefits."

"Maybe I'll give it a try, but a month is really all that I have. After that, I should be back in Epoch."

"Here, let me help you." She got up and stood behind him. "Now close your eyes and try to calm your mind while you control your breathing like I showed you." She put her hands on his shoulders and immediately felt his warmth, passion, and strength flow through her. This was unlike anything she had felt before, and she lingered in the sensation, letting her emotions wrap around her.

"Concentrate on that breathing, think of nothing else," she said, slowly caressing his shoulders.

He could concentrate on nothing but her hands. Her slow massage was both relaxing and sensual, causing his nerves to tingle in waves from head to toe. He felt a subconscious connection to her and could sense her calmness, confidence, and quite unexpectedly, her strong feelings for him.

When she finally removed her hands, he opened his eyes, and to his own surprise, found that the sun had set.

He looked up at her and smiled. "How long were we like that?" he asked.

She tried to think, lost in her own thoughts. "About an hour, I guess."

He rose and looked into her eyes, knowing that something extraordinary had just occurred, and he felt guilty as though he had cheated on Allison.

"You can sense animals, can't you?" Lauren asked. She wanted to change the subject.

"What do you mean, 'sense'?"

"You can sense when they're watching you, and maybe sense other emotions within them," she replied.

"A few strange things have happened over the last year or so," he explained, "and when I was hiking after the plane crash, I did get the feeling that a raven was watching me."

"It's a good thing you can feel these things—otherwise, I'm sure a wolf or cougar would've eaten you for supper when you spent those nights in the forest after the crash. We should work on this in our next session. I think we can perfect that skill though it would've been better to start when you were much younger." She smiled at him and turned to head back to her hut.

Alec's mind was whirling as he followed her back. There had been a powerful connection between them while he meditated and during their talk about sensing animals. *Sensing animals may be real after all! I'm going to need some good proof before I tell Dad about any of this, or he'll think I've gone crazy.*

****

Jordan sat in Jake's office listening intently to every word spoken by the city manager. At first, he could hardly contain his excitement when the commander had told him that he would be leading the Little Bear Lake squad. His initial enthusiasm was curbed in the following days as he realized how much preparation would be needed. There was the selection of the other team members, organizing the supplies necessary for such a long journey, and now he was sitting in Jake's office listening to additional instructions.

"Jordan, we need to make this a quick strike mission," Jake directed. "I want you up there in under three weeks and then to make short work of draining that lake and getting to the structure. Review the team that you're going up with, and make sure you can trust everyone. And for God's sake, make sure that Clyde isn't one of them."

Laughing at the reference to Clyde, Jordan said, "Yes, sir, I can do that. Are you worried about Percipience getting to it before we do?"

Jake smiled. Jordan was proving to be better than he had hoped. He was eager and seemed to have a knack for dealing with people and understanding situations. "Yes, that's exactly the reason. I can't stress enough how important it is for us to get there first, and I want you to use any means necessary. Am I making myself clear?"

"Yes, sir," Jordan acknowledged, and then added, "I'll make sure that in addition to the food supplies we're adequately armed to handle whatever comes up." He outlined details of the plans he had already made and was surprised that Jake offered only a few minor changes. As he was about to leave, he noticed a drawing of a city that he did not recognize.

"Where is this?" he asked.

"Those are my initial plans for our new satellite village. The one that we're going to build right beside Percipience."

"I thought that the plans were for one south of here? Is their leader, Robert, in favor of this?"

"Why wouldn't he be? This will expand the economy for both of us and we'll have lots of salvageable materials from nearby Coppertown to help us with its construction. If you play your cards right, you could be one of the leaders in this new town."

"Really?"

"Of course! Let's talk more about it after you return."

Jordan left the office brimming with confidence and set off to finish the last of the preparations for his mission.

12 - THE JOURNEY

It had been more than three days since Robert had heard from the team at Little Bear, and he was getting worried. The last report that they sent indicated they were making good progress, and that the tip of the pyramid was now above the water. They would need another week or so of controlled explosions on the dam to get the water level to the pyramid's base.

He wanted to go up to the site himself to find out what had happened and then had an idea that would solve a few problems at the same time. He found Alec and Lauren and told them about the Percipience team and his concerns about not hearing from them recently.

"What do you think could've gone wrong?" Alec asked.

"Could be several things—from a simple problem with the radio to something far more serious, like an accident with the explosives. They did take a fair amount along with them. But if it were a radio problem, one of them should've started back and would be here by now. That's why I'm concerned."

"Can we send up a runner to check on them?" Lauren asked.

"Already done. I sent up the young lad that beat you in The Run during the last Games. He should be there no later than tomorrow morning".

"Yeah, and I'm surprised he's not there already considering his speed and endurance. Maybe we should think about going up as well."

To her surprise, Robert had the same thought. "We could leave tomorrow and take an easy walk up there. I'd feel better starting now instead of waiting another three weeks like we'd planned."

Not waiting for her father to change his mind, she led Alec off to pack a few things, leaving Robert on his own. His idea had worked perfectly, and Lauren had taken the bait. He felt relieved that Alec would be a step closer to going home, and that Lauren would be out of Percipience, enabling the elders to work on validating his calculations without fear of her discovering them.

The following morning, the three of them began the journey with several other men from Percipience. Using a cane for support, Alec did his best to keep up with the others, but the pace was still slow, and it took them a few days to reach the location where Alec had made his emergency landing. Robert's concern for the team at Little Bear increased when they lost radio communication with the runner he had sent.

The plane was exactly as Alec had left it with one of its floaters wedged on a log. He remembered the landing and the work it had taken to secure the plane. A few hundred yards in either direction would have resulted in his crashing into the trees or large rocks that protruded from the water at the mouth of the river.

"You fly in the air in that thing?" Lauren asked. "I was expecting something much bigger and something . . . well . . . safer looking. It looks really fragile."

"She's very sturdy and reliable."

"And that's why you crashed?"

He ignored her comment and walked away to where her father stood. "My friend, Jordan, and I build this from scratch, including the engine. Before the Great Loss, it would've been easy, but with the limited knowledge, tools, and materials we have today it was a pile of work."

"Impressive," Robert said. "But what caused you to come down?"

"I think it was a crack in the cylinder head that caused a lack of compression in the engine and all sorts of other problems. Here, I'll show you." He walked towards the plane. They spent the remaining part of the afternoon together examining the engine while the others set up camp for the night. "It looks like we have a badly cracked cylinder head and a timing chain that has seen better days," said Alec. "I think we'll have to go with our second plan. I'll go back via horseback when the Epoch team gets to the pyramid."

"Not so fast," Robert said. "We may be able to rebuild those things for you."

"You can make a cylinder head and new links for this chain? I didn't see anything more complex than a shower head and a radiator in your village."

"I didn't say it would be easy, but I'm pretty sure that we can do it," Robert said. "Let's get these parts off of the plane, and we'll give it a try. A few days won't make any real difference if it turns out we can't repair them. In the meantime, you, Lauren, and I can find out what's happening at the pyramid and with my team."

"True enough," Alec said. They used the plane's toolkit to remove the parts. When they were finished, they headed to the newly made camp, and Alec was impressed. In a short time, the others had built a shelter, started a fire, and were preparing the evening meal, which was rehydrated potatoes, wild carrots and berries, and two freshly caught trout.

"Smells great!" Alec told Lauren as she was putting a bit of seasoning on the trout.

"I think so too— the guys were lucky to catch a few fish for tonight. Otherwise, I was thinking of some nice cooked grasshoppers."

His face didn't hide his feelings. "I'm glad they caught some fish too. I'm barely getting used to grubs and things buried in my food. I don't think I could look a bug in the eye and gobble it up."

After dinner, Lauren left the group and sat on the ground at the edge of the lake. A mist had started to come in, and she could no longer see the other side but could make out the half moon. She had started to clear her mind and get focused when she heard footsteps approaching. Alec settled himself on the ground near her.

“Mind if I join you?”

“Do I have a choice?” She laughed. “I was actually going to do a bit of meditation. I want a clear head for tomorrow when we get to that pyramid.’

“It’ll do you good to skip it occasionally and simply enjoy the moment, or a beautiful view like this." He reached over and put his hand on hers.

His touch sent shivers through her. *Every time he’s near me, my heart skips a beat. I’ve never felt like this around anyone else.* She quickly recovered. “I’ll give you that—it’s quite a view. I spend a lot of time up this way. My wolf and the rest of his pack have their den on the other side of the hill." She pointed downstream.

“Tell me more about that wolf. It’s like you can read each other’s mind."

“It’s not really mind reading, I just sense how he’s feeling, and I’m pretty sure he has the same connection with me. It’s been like that since he was a pup—kind of like when you’re sensing animals, but to a higher degree."

“Having the feeling of being watched is one thing, but sensing their feelings, that’s impossible,” Alec argued. “There’s no evidence in any of the reading I’ve done that indicates any kind of interspecies communication or telepathy or anything like that is possible."

“No, there’s actually a lot of evidence," she said, “but prior to the Great Loss, it wasn’t accepted by the scientific community. They couldn’t reproduce it with their crude tests, and they had no viable theories of its possibility. So this and several other things, like telekinesis, or pre-cognition of future events and the like, were deemed impossible."

“All of that is fringe science. I just don’t believe in any of it."

Lauren looked at him for a moment and shook her head. She turned back to face the lake, and the water began to swell.

“What?” he started to say and then saw a shape form in the swell, crude at first, but quickly refined. The shape of a wolf appeared and suddenly lunged at him.

He screamed and tried to scramble up to his feet but was immersed in water as the shape collapsed around him.

“Impossible, huh?” She got up and started back to the campsite.

She had taken only a few steps and heard her father.

“What happened? What was the screaming about?” he asked as he approached.

Alec was about to reply but then noticed the stern look on Lauren’s face.

“The city boy just fell into the lake, that’s all.”

Alec played along despite not understanding her motive. “Yeah, my leg gave out, and I guess I need to get these clothes dry. He got up and followed them back to the camp.

The next morning, Robert sent some of the men back to Percipience with the broken plane parts while he, Alec, and Lauren and the rest of the team continued their adventure to Little Bear.

“Lauren, about last night," Alec said, “How did you do that?”

“I don’t want to talk about it right now." She felt angry with herself for losing control and disobeying her father by showing Alec her powers.

“There’s no way I can forget that," he said.

"You will, your mind doesn't have any choice. It can't explain it, and even after this conversation, after a while you won't be able to tell if it happened or not. Now, let's get packed up—we need to get to the pyramid site."

He felt confused but agreed to drop the subject for the time being and helped her pack their gear.

Between the rough terrain and his inability to move at full speed, it was past noon before they got to the top of the small mountain that separated Bear Lake from Little Bear. As they came over the crest, they were greeted by the remarkable sight of trees and hills that merged as far as the eye could see into the distant mountain range. They looked down into the valley where there had once been a lake, now was only a mud-covered expanse. The pyramid stood, quite out of place, at its center atop a large, cement slab.

Even at a distance, the four white sides appeared to be in perfect condition rising to meet at the top, which was covered with a golden cap that reflected the sunlight. Lauren and Alec were mesmerized by the structure while Robert looked for signs of his men. He immediately noticed something out of place. Near the pyramid, where the shore of the lake had been, several men were engaged in activity. Tents had been set up, and horses drank or grazed nearby.

"Looks like your father forgot to tell us that the Epoch team made it here early." Robert's voice was etched with sarcasm. "I wonder what they did to my men."

He moved quickly as they headed down the hill towards the campsite. They approached the shoreline and were greeted by a couple of men that Robert did not recognize. The men quickly raised their rifles, and when Robert continued to stride towards them, one of the men fired a warning shot that landed a few feet in front of him. He understood that these young men with rifles may be nervous enough to shoot him, and he stopped.

Alec did not recognize either of the men, but the warning shot had alerted others, and soon they were surrounded by a dozen armed men a few of whom did recognize him.

A man who appeared to be the leader came forward. "Alec! It's good to see you!"

"Put down the guns," Alec replied, "There's no need for them."

"Orders are orders, and I'm not going to break them," the young man said. "A couple of us will escort you to the command tent, but the rest of you will be having a visit with your friends."

Robert sized up the situation. There were two other men from Percipience still with him plus Lauren. He and the other men were at least a foot taller than the men from Epoch and appeared in much better physical form. He was certain they could easily win a fight, but the Epoch team had guns, and that tipped the scales considerably. He signaled his team to do as they were told, and they were led down the hill towards the tents.

Alec was separated from them and led towards one of the smaller tents. At the same time, Robert and Lauren and the rest of the Percipience team were escorted into to a large tent nearby.

"I'll get this straightened out as soon as I can," Alec called back to them as he was led away.

"I should've anticipated this," Robert said to Lauren as they entered the tent. They recognized the men from Percipience including the runner who had arrived earlier.

"What happened?" Robert asked. His anger faded to relief seeing his men were unharmed.

"They showed up about five days ago," one of the men said. "There was really not much we could do—they far outnumbered us and had rifles. They rounded us up and put us in this tent. They've taken good care of us, but took our radio, and within a day of being here, they put a pile of explosives at the dam and blew a huge hole in it. The lake drained very quickly."

“They’re idiots," said Robert. “Who knows how much damage was done downstream with the flood waters that must have come through with the explosion.”

The man who had reported the events began to laugh softly.

“What’s so funny?

“I think they may be having a bit of a trouble. For the last few days we’ve been hearing frantic conversations coming from their command tent. At first they were pleased with themselves for getting the lake drained so quickly, but now they’re stuck.”

“Stuck?” Lauren repeated.

“Yeah," the man said with a grin. “They’ve worked around the clock for the last four days, but they still haven’t figured out how to get inside the pyramid."

13 - PROGRESS

Jake was both surprised and pleased to hear from Jordan earlier than planned. The long distance between Epoch and Little Bear lake made portable radios useless so Jordan's team had brought along a more powerful base transmitter, antenna, and batteries which they setup upon arriving.

"Great progress, Jordan," Jake said.

"There were a few people here from Percipience, but we contained them quickly." Jordan reported. "No serious injuries and I have them under guard in one of the tents. It looks like they were trying to drain the lake slowly, but I knew that you wanted this done fast, so I had our team place most of the explosives we brought, plus what the Percipience team had, at the base of the dam. It was quite an explosion and it blew a gigantic hole in it. The lake is draining rapidly now, and we should be at the base of the pyramid within a day."

"Excellent. I didn't make a bad choice putting you in charge." Jake could almost feel Jordan's pride coming from the radio. "Oh, by the way, there was a horrible accident here a few days ago. The commander was driving out to a guard tower in the military truck proto-type, and it looks like the brakes failed as he was going down a hill. It flipped over and killed him instantly. So until we can find a suitable replacement for him, the elected officials have put me in charge of the DC."

"My God, that's awful! I'm so sorry—We're all very fortunate to have you there to take over, Jake."

The accidental death of the high-profile commander was a big shock to the people of Epoch. Jake immediately ordered an inspection of the other proto-type vehicles and organized one of the largest ceremonies that Epoch had ever had to honor the commander's life. After the ceremony, he convinced the elected officials that no suitable replacement could be found among the full-time DC members and volunteered to be Acting commander until they found someone. They were more than happy to go along with his plan as they knew the people of Epoch trusted Jake, and it would defer them from having to make a decision.

"Keep me updated on the progress you're making," he told Jordan before signing off. "Let nothing prevent you from getting inside that structure."

"Yes, sir!"

Jake's first stop afterward was a meeting with Allison and Kimberly to review progress on the oil refinery. He also wanted to go to the DC to initiate some of the changes he wanted made now that he was in charge. *Another six months and I will be the permanent commander of the DC.* He exited the town hall building and climbed into his new truck.

The sound of Jake's truck starting shattered the tranquility of the downtown area, and the main street cleared quickly of people. Vehicles were still a novelty, and everyone usually stopped what they were doing to witness one going by. Word had quickly spread, however, that it would be better to watch Jake from a good distance, and preferably from a location that offered sturdy protection. Even the truck shuddered as it idled roughly until he ground the gears to get it into first and punched the gas, causing the vehicle to lurch ahead onto the street.

He enjoyed the attention as he drove down the middle of the main street with people frantically waving and pointing at him. He honked the horn several times while looking out of the side window at the crowd and waving back. As he leaned to one side to see the other side of the street, he unintentionally looked in the direction that the truck was heading. He could see the horrified look of the people standing in a tram car that had stopped in the middle of the road just a hundred feet in front of him.

He tried to put his foot over the brake pedal, but it slipped onto the accelerator causing the truck to leap forward. Seeing no other option, he turned the steering wheel as hard as he could, which caused the truck to bounce over the curb and onto the sidewalk in front of the warehouse. The guards at the entrance doors made a hasty retreat as the truck slid within a few feet of them. He swerved it back onto the road ahead of the tram. The truck veered a few more times before he got things under control and headed away from the town center towards the refinery.

He pulled up right on time and was greeted by Kimberly and Allison.

"How's the truck?" Allison asked as he climbed out.

"Love it!" he exclaimed with a boyish grin

Kimberly pointed to a small branch hanging off the passenger mirror. "What happened? Did a tree jump out in front of you?" Allison quipped.

"Something like that," Jake admitted. "I'll get better with more experience. For new drivers, I've talked the elected officials into passing a law requiring that a test be taken before people can drive on their own. Of course, I made sure that existing drivers like me will be grandfathered in and won't need to." He winked as they headed into the building complex.

Kimberly acted as tour guide as they toured the refinery. "It's a pretty simple facility and not quite finished yet, but we're producing enough fuel for the few vehicles in the DC and around town. We've also just filled up a fuel truck that's going out to the highway construction team."

"Have we got all the old vehicles refurbished now—from before the Loss?" he asked. Although a great deal of care was taken when putting them into storage, there were several parts that did not make the nearly two-hundred-year wait.

"The highway foreman says that he has enough equipment now to do the job," Allison replied. "We're still making more rubber feedstock, but not all of that is going to parts for the earth movers anymore. Some of it is making its way to the other factories and shops around town because there are endless uses for it."

"Excellent! How about the capacity of the refinery when it's finished?"

"It can handle a quite a bit more oil than we're getting from this well," she said.

"I already have some longer-term plans for that." He pointed to workers making their way back and forth along a catwalk. "Why are they wearing gas masks?"

"Yeah—it's not the healthiest place to be around, we don't have all the technology built yet for really good air or wastewater filtration. To be safe, the people who work are required to wear them."

"Then I'm glad that we built this downwind and downstream from Epoch," he said, not giving it a second thought. "The Re-Discovery Center has come through well on this project. Once it's finalized, we'll need to change the focus to electronics."

Kimberly interrupted before he could go on. "I thought we were going to concentrate on building some of the pollution controls—like what's needed in this factory, or the coal generator, and even the vehicles. Wasn't that was one of major platforms used in winning the last election?"

He had been caught off guard but rebounded quickly, "Well, yes, we'll have to work on that, but in order to get the real growth we should first get a better handle on the electronics."

Having little control of what they worked on, Allison and Kimberly already suspected what kind of priority that pollution control would get and shrugged at each other.

After the refinery tour, Jake went back to his truck, pulled the branch from the passenger mirror, and drove to the DC to meet with his newly appointed manager of daily operations. As he passed through the main gates, he barely avoided colliding with a team of horses pulling a wagon out of the complex. He steered off the road, sending a training squad scrambling for cover, and after a few erratic turns found the brakes in time to stop in front of the main office.

As Jake let himself out of the truck, a young man came running from the building. "Are you okay, sir?" he asked, surveying the carnage left behind.

"Of course, why do you ask? And, by the way, from now on, all animals, wagons and the like are to only use the side gate. We want to leave the main gate only for motorized vehicles."

"Yes, sir!" He saw that Jake's truck was the only motorized vehicle around, but decided against pointing it out.

He entered the office building and started to go over troop assignments and training programs with the soldier in charge. "This will never do!" Jake said. "We need more soldiers, especially if we need to take military action with Percipience."

"The commander tried to get more recruits, but had little success," the young man said.

"Well, now that I'm in charge, things are going to be different. In honor of the late commander, I've convinced the council to realign the budget and reduce funding from education and seniors' programs and put more towards the DC. They're allowing me to re-organize some of the factory work too so that we can build the convoy trucks that the commander wanted and some more rifles and other firearms."

"Fantastic news, sir. I'm sure the late commander would've been impressed at the actions you're taking."

"All in his memory, son!" Jake replied, slapping him on the back. "Now, I must get going. Start preparing schedules for more boot camps—we're going to need them!"

Jake whistled happily when he got back into his truck feeling pleased with how things were progressing. He could see the pieces of the plan coming together as he started his truck. *Nobody suspects a thing.*

14 - THE PUZZLE

Alec could hardly believe his eyes as his escorts forced him towards a tent with armed guards at the entry. Inside, he knew instantly that this was the center of operation. There were foldout tables holding maps, papers, and a radio transmitter. At the rear of the tent, he was shocked and bewildered to see Jordan sitting behind what was clearly the command desk.

"Jordan!" he shouted impulsively. "What are you doing here, and what's going on?" He started towards Jordan's desk. The guard standing in the rear corner of the tent leapt into action.

"Alec!" Jordan rose from his chair, motioning for the guard to stand down. He rushed from behind his desk to greet his friend.

Alec jumped back before Jordan reached him. "What are all these guns for, and why are the people from Percipience being held as prisoner here? You have to let them go!"

The two men stood facing one another awkwardly in a moment of angry silence. Jordan held his hands up in a pleading gesture. "Hold on, Alec, this is your dad's plan. He put me in charge of this squad to make sure that whatever is in that pyramid gets to Epoch and not to Percipience."

Alec sighed, knowing this was exactly the kind of action his father would organize. "Then let's get on the radio and see if we can change his mind."

They shortly were explaining the situation to Jake, who started his response with a soft laugh.

"You've done a good job, Jordan, but locking up one of the leaders of Percipience may have been a bit over the top. Let's let them all go—that will free up the guards, and maybe they can help us figure out how to get into that pyramid."

Alec looked over at Jordan, "You haven't been inside yet?"

"No. Whoever built that thing put in a puzzle and the threat of a booby trap if we don't solve it first." He pressed the transmitter key. "Okay, sir, we'll get right on it. I'll keep you updated if anything changes here."

"Good," Jake said, "But, remember, the intent of my original orders still stands. I want whatever is found inside to be brought back to Epoch."

"Understand, sir," Jordan responded and signed off. He barked a command to the nearest guard to release the Percipience team. He and Alec left the tent and walked the short distance to the drained lake. They gazed at the pyramid that stood before them. A stream of water flowed by it, following the original river path there before the landslide that formed the lake.

"I wonder who made it." Alec said.

"Who knows—there's no reference to it anywhere. We've had people at the Re-Discovery Center scour through the libraries, and nothing came up. There are plaques beside it, though, saying it was built in 2022, just before the Great Loss."

"Are you in charge here?" an angry voice asked. Jordan felt a hand tapping on his shoulder.

"Yes, Sir," Jordan said as he turned and extended his hand. *This man is a giant, just like the rest of the men from Percipience.* "You must be Robert. I apologize for my overzealous guards. They were only doing what was they thought was right."

"Why do you have guards to begin with, and why did you take members from my village prisoner?"

"They were not prisoners, sir," Jordan said, "I wanted to make sure they were safe while we did our explosive work."

Robert stared at him and knew he was lying, but he had calmed down enough to realize that nothing would be gained from starting a fight, especially with this young man. He would save his rage for the next time he spoke to Jake.

Alec tugged at Jordan's jacket. "I'd like you to meet my doctor, Lauren." He smiled as she came up and stood by her father.

Thankful for the distraction, Jordan smiled as he looked at her and Robert.

"I'm pleased to meet you," he said looking at Lauren, "I was expecting someone much older with a large wart on their nose." He leaned towards Alec. "And I guess a few other people in Epoch are expecting the same thing," he whispered.

Lauren paid little attention to Jordan, her gaze fixed on the pyramid. "I'm going to look at that," she said.

Alec replied to Jordan in a hushed voice. "I know," he said. "I'm not sure how I'm going to handle it, but right now, I'm going to look at the pyramid too."

"I'll join you two in a while," said Robert. "I need to sort out a few things here first and then make sure the rest of our team is all right." He looked at Jordan. "I'm going to try and forget about the past few hours. Let's work together and get this figured out." He pointed to the pyramid. "Assuming you have a radio here that I can use, I want to contact Percipience and let them know what's going on. There's been no communication from my team for a few days, and people over there are getting worried."

"Sure," Jordan said and led him back to the command tent. Robert told him about the plane parts that needed to be repaired and that they had been shipped to Percipience. Jordan set up the radio for him then left to catch up with Alec. He signaled to a few guards to watch over Robert.

Lauren and Alec moved quickly, and Jordan finally caught up to them as they looked at a plaque bolted into the rock by the pyramid. Beside the plaque, there was a large wheel with a pointer on it, and surrounding it on the rock was a series of numbers like a dial counting from one to nine. They read the writing on the plaque.

Within this structure is great power and treasure
Along with some puzzles for your solving pleasure
Attempting to get in without solving these riddles
Will toast the inside as if on a griddle
The walls hold the key - not as easy as it seems
You will need more than eyes to achieve this dream

Good Luck!

Time Capsule #3, August 24, 2022

“A poem!” Alec said in surprise. “Puzzle, treasure . . . what’s going on here, and what’s this wheel about?”

“Oh, that’s the best part—watch this," Jordan said. He put both hands on the wheel and turned it half way so that it pointed to the number five, and then let it go. Nothing happened.

“What’s that for?”

“Wait," Jordan said. Fifteen minutes passed, and the wheel slowly turned back to the “one” position and stopped.

“This is too much,” Alec said. “Who would build such a thing?”

“I’m not sure, but there’s more. There are four of these, one on each side of the pyramid and each written in a different language—English, French, Hebrew, and Chinese. The behavior of the wheels is the same too. If we turn any combination of them, after fifteen minutes from the last turn, all four of the wheels turn back to the “one” position.

“Obviously, some kind of combination," Alec said. “And clever, too, because for a four-digit combination with a fifteen-minute delay, just guessing the combination would take months. Based on that date, it must’ve been completed right around the time of the Great Loss.”

“That’s what I was thinking," Jordan said. “I’ve been tempted to break in, but with the warning on the plaque, I’m afraid that if we do, whatever is inside will be destroyed."

They spent the rest of the afternoon exploring the pyramid and looking for more clues and attempted a few combinations that didn’t work. Later that evening, Lauren and Alec sat on the lake shore, a fire crackling behind them as they looked out over the mud towards the pyramid.

“So, Alec, what kind of power and treasure do you think would have been put in there? I doubt if it’s gold or anything like that. It would be pretty useless to anyone who found it.”

“I don’t know. There could be gold in there. Gold has been used for currency in every age—we even use it in Epoch."

“You have money in Epoch?” she asked.

"Of course, how else would people get paid for their work, or buy things? You need money to have specialization and growth."

Lauren gave him a confused look. She picked up a stick and began to gently prod at a nearby anthill. "I can't find any—can you see some?"

"See what?"

"I’m looking for their money," she said. "They have separation of duties, gather food, raise young ants, build wondrous structures, and even defend them." She put the stick down and placed a few berries near it as a peace offering to the ants that were starting to climb up the stick.

"But they’re just ants! They don’t have any personal possessions."

"So you need money to buy things other than food and shelter?" she asked. Do you pay for food in Epoch?"

"Well, of course. The people that grow and prepare the food need money to buy the things they need."

“In Percipience, food is grown in my hut, and then we give it to the people in other huts,” she said. They don’t pay for it, and even if they did, I don’t know what I’d do with money. What would I need or want to buy?”

Alec shook his head, knowing that the concept was incomprehensible to her. “Someday when you visit Epoch, you’ll see.” He wanted to change the subject and looked back out at the pyramid. “Maybe it’s a new power source or a weapon."

“Power source maybe, but I doubt a weapon," she said, relieved to be off the subject of money as well. “I just don’t think that someone would create something as beautiful as this and then fill it with guns. What would be the point? I’m more interested in finding the clues. We’ve looked over all the walls, and there are no symbols.”

“I know—so many questions! I wonder if the plaques all say the same thing, or if there are different clues in the different languages.”

They debated about the combination for several days. Some of the numbers tried were based on the pyramid dimensions, the number of tiles, and the year it was built. The results were always the same: the wheels turned back to their starting position, and no entrance to the pyramid was revealed.

After another long day of futile attempts, they felt mentally exhausted and returned to their campsite. Jordan and Robert were already there involved in a heated discussion.

Jordan believed that no harm could come from drilling a hole through the wall. “If we can get a look inside then we can figure out how to bypass whatever traps are in there.”

"And at the same time you could destroy whatever is inside," Robert said, "There's no rush to get in. Why not simply try all of the combinations? Within a year we'd get it."

"A year!" Jordan's patience had run out, and his voice reached across the campsite. "We're not waiting a whole year to get in. Jake wants us to be inside within the next two days, or I'm ordered to get in by force."

"I don't care what Jake wants. The same rash decisions and actions caused unknown amounts of damage when you blew up the dam." Before Jordan could respond, Robert got up and stormed away.

Jordan looked at Alec and Lauren, who had stayed silent witnesses to the argument. "Two days," he said, "and if we're not in by then, I have my orders." He walked off angrily in the direction of the command tent.

"I agree with my Dad," Lauren said. "I'm dying to find out what's inside, but we really shouldn't rush it."

"You haven't met my Dad yet. He's not that patient, and if Jordan doesn't do as he's told, Dad will find someone who will."

"I guess we'll just have to figure out this puzzle in the next two days then," she said. "And to do that, we need to stop thinking about it for a while and gather up some food."

They combed the area around the edge of the old lake and returned within an hour with a harvest of mushrooms, cattails, berries, and some edible plants that Alec didn't recognize. Shortly afterward, Lauren handed him a plate of prepared food that he finished to the last berry. *She can go anywhere and live off the land. Amazing.* He thought about how much work people had to do in Epoch to earn enough money to buy food. Here, it wasn't an issue. Within a few weeks, the supplies that Jordan's squad had brought with them would be exhausted. With no knowledge of foraging for food, they would be obliged to return. He wondered why Epoch was the way it was.

After their meal, they sat back and watched the reflection of the flames dance over the pyramid. The image was a shifting silhouette against an evening sky full of stars. "Maybe we shouldn't try to get inside," she said. "During my meditations, I've had troublesome thoughts about the pyramid, though I'm not sure what they all meant."

"We *have* to get inside," he said. "Until we do, I doubt if I'll be able to think of much else. Are you rethinking the possibility of weapons inside?"

"Still doubt it," she said, "I wonder though." She unhooked her radiation meter and looked at it. The single green dot showed that nothing was being detected. "Come along," she said.

When they arrived at the pyramid, she walked around it. A second green dot flickered on and off intermittently. "Hey, Alec, come over here!"

"What is it?"

"This talk of weapons makes me think that maybe there was some kind of nuclear thing inside. Look at my radiation meter—if I stand here, it's normal, but if I move slightly, the second light starts to flicker. I don't know if it means anything."

"Several people have already checked for radiation coming from it but haven't found anything abnormal," Alec said.

"But this meter is very sensitive. And look, even a few feet away from the wall, nothing, but if I hold it up against the wall at this one spot, the second green dot flickers."

She handed him the meter, and he repeated the same movements and noticed the same behavior in the lights. Then he put the meter on the pyramid again and began to slide it across the wall. The single green light was on, and the second light appeared without flickering. As he continued to push it across the marble surface, the second light went off again. They moved the detector across the expanse of the wall and only in certain places did the second light come on consistently.

"What do you think?" she asked.

"Not sure—let's trace the area where this second light comes on." With only moonlight, they spent the next hour sliding the meter over the wall and used charcoal from the campfire to trace where the meter had shown a higher reading. When they were done, they stepped back and saw a perfectly shaped "L" on the marble wall.

"We got it!" he shouted. "There must be a small radioactive source right under the wall with lead shielding or something that focuses the outbound radiation."

They were too excited to stop and worked into the night, repeating the procedure on the other walls. After several hours, they had traced the letters L, two I's and an X

"I wonder what it's supposed to mean?" he asked.

"Impossible to know. She felt equally frustrated. "But I do know that I'm tired. Let's get some sleep, and we can tell the others about this in the morning."

They didn't rest long. Their discovery from the previous night held new excitement, and at the first sounds of people stirring with the morning sunrise, they rose to tell Robert and Jordan what they had found.

A burst of activity was triggered by the news. There was a new level of anticipation within the camp as people tried to decode the letters. Jordan relayed the information to Epoch hoping that Allison and Kimberly might be able to help using reference material from the Re-Discovery Center.

Lauren and Alec found nothing more after a second trip to examine the walls. They went back to the command tent to see if any progress had been made.

"None yet," Jordan said, "Kimberly and Allison will be calling back to let us know what they have found."

"Hopefully, there'll be something to tell us," Alec said. "Did your men find anything else? We noticed one soldier out in the middle of the muddy part of the lake bed, and he's been there all day."

Jordan scowled "That was the soldier who did the initial radiation scan on the pyramid and told me there was nothing."

"But the signal was weak. Even my detector had to be right against the wall to pick it up." Lauren said.

"No excuse. He should've found it, and now he's getting more practice."

"Practice?" Alec asked.

"I told him that I buried one of our radiation detector calibration blocks out there." Jordan pointed to where the soldier trudged through the mud. "He's not to come back until he finds it."

"Is the calibration block near where he is now?" Lauren asked.

"No. I never put one out there. I'll let him look through the night and sometime tomorrow I'll call him back in."

15 - DISCOVERY

Late in the afternoon, Jordan, Alec, and Lauren were at the radio listening to Kimberly.

“Assuming these are Roman numerals, our best guess is 5111, which would be the numerals written out and then dropping the zeros since you don’t have any on the wheels. And we don’t know if it’s important, but the only way to combine all the characters into a single Roman number is XLII, which represents 42.”

With some doubt, they went to the pyramid and tried the 5111 combination. They didn’t know which wheel to start with, and they tried all four, which took more than an hour. The result was always the same: the wheels became reset. They tried “4242” with the same disappointing result.

It was getting dark, and there was little further activity except for flute music played by a member of the Percipience team. Alec and Lauren sat by themselves at their campfire listening to the distant music and the evening sounds of the forest. She idly sketched symbols in the sand with a stick. She played with the numbers and tried to rearrange the lines to no avail. Then she scratched “42” into the sand and paused.

“It couldn’t be … could it?”

“What are you thinking?”

She paused again before answering and looked at the numbers. “We know that the pyramid is recent, maybe only a few hundred years old and that whoever built it has a kind of a twisted sense of purpose with the silly poem and puzzle. If the symbols are Roman numerals, and they represent the number 42, maybe there’s a riddle in that. Maybe it’s not 42, but four twos.”

He laughed. "You mean like 2222? Hey, why not? Let’s give it a try.”

They went back to the pyramid and set all the wheels to the number two and waited, expecting them to reset again. Instead, they felt a small tremor underneath them and then nothing. They looked at each other in anticipation and confusion.

"Did you feel that?" he asked.

"Yes. I wonder what's supposed to happen now."

A soft thud came from the other side of the pyramid. They raced towards it and found that a section of the marble wall the size of a large door had collapsed into the pyramid forming an entry ramp up.

They shouted simultaneously and gave each other a hug. They clung to each other as they looked up the ramp. Alec turned to look at Lauren and gave into his emotions by giving her a passionate kiss before they drew apart. Lauren felt her heart racing. She put her head against Alec's chest and could hear his speeding heartbeat. They stood together in silence, delighting in the moment. Finally, he broke the spell. "After you," he whispered, gesturing towards the ramp that led up into the pyramid.

"I think we'll need a bit of light," she said, her thoughts still swirling. She was reluctant to let go.

He gently broke free and ran to their campfire returning with a lit branch to use as a torch.

With their torch, they went up the ramp and at the end could see what looked like a door made of metal with a handle on it. To their surprise, the inside of the ramp and the door felt dry giving them hope that whatever was inside had not been damaged by the water.

They reached for the handle, gave it a turn, and pushed. With the flickering flame of their torch, they peered inside and could make out crates and boxes in the room. She noticed a crank handle on the wall beside the door. Beside the crank, there was an arrow indicating which way to turn it and the marking "20X" beside it the arrow.

"This looks like it wants us to turn the crank twenty times—should we give it a try?" she asked.

He reached for the crank. "Why not?"

Despite its age, it turned smoothly. After five turns, they noticed a dim light, and when he had turned it twenty times, the room, though not bright, was noticeably brighter. He put the torch down outside the pyramid, and they entered the room. It was smaller than they expected, measuring about fifteen feet square. They saw several crates stacked against the walls. In the middle of the room was a large, clear plastic enclosure, and within that, a simple desk with four neatly arranged stacks of thin metal plates on it.

As they walked around the enclosed desk, they saw that the stacks of plates contained writing in different languages, like the plaques outside. They read the English plate.

WISE

(Weblike Intelligent Search Engine)

Assembly and Operating Instructions

On one of the walls, they found a world map with lines connecting several points, and four buttons, each with a language label above it. Alec immediately pressed the button under the English label. The lights dimmed, and then a voice emanating from the ceiling was heard.

"Welcome to my little treasure trove. My name is Richard. I've built a few of these around the globe and am very happy that this one has been discovered. I don't know the current year, but this site was constructed in 2022, and the crates around you contain a simple computer system and a vast library of indestructible information discs, or at least that's what my engineers tell me. The system is nicknamed WISE, and there is information on history, arts, and science, and several other fields. They should assist you in speeding your recovery, and hopefully, to avoid the mistakes made by the culture that I was a part of. If you have read about the Internet from my time, this is very similar, with nearly instant access to any information you may want. Instruction sheets are on the desk before you, which is encased, as are all the crates, in an argon-filled environment to ensure that there is no decay."

"You may be curious about the radio signal that led you to this structure and why I have done all of this. I am the founder of the villages near these sites. I built them since I fear that some type of major collapse may occur soon that will plunge the world into chaos. To prepare for this, I constructed the villages along with guidelines for a way to live that will be more in harmony with the planet and each other. I have set the radio signals to start to broadcast 150 years after the last satellite signal is detected and they lead you to here. Why not put WISE in the villages to begin with? I feel that it is critical to let the villages have several generations to get used to the new way of life first. After this has been engrained they will be able to use the information held within WISE to enhance this lifestyle instead of just going back to a consumption based culture."

"I hope everything has worked out as I have planned and the best of luck to you."

They looked at each other in awe. "Wow . . . can you imagine what this could do?" Alec exlaimed. "This will change everything. We're spending so much time re-inventing things, and now, everything will be at our fingertips!"

She felt lightheaded, and her throat was dry. "This is going to be more valuable than anything on the planet. I don't think we should open anything now. Let's wait until we get my dad and Jordan in here."

"Then let's wake them up now!" He started towards the door.

****

Soon after the discovery, all four stood together in the pyramid room. Alec recounted how they solved the puzzle, and what happened when the combination was entered. They replayed the recording, and when it was over, an eerie quiet settled around them, each lost in thought.

Jordan was excited and worried. Like everyone else, he understood the immense gift that this meant, but at the same time, his practical side recognized that there was no way he could move the large amount of boxes safely back to Epoch.

Robert quickly realized this too.

"Well, Jordan, it seems like you have a bit of a problem if you're thinking of moving all of this."

"Uh . . . yes, I'm not sure quite what we should do. But we can't leave it all just sitting here, and the road to Coppertown won't be ready for months. Even when it is finished, it is still quite some ways from here."

Robert could see Jordan's inexperience and offered his advice. "We could bring them to Percipience, and you could use it there. Let's talk to Jake in the morning. We don't need to make any decisions tonight."

Jordan felt relieved at the thought of deferring the decision to Jake. The idea of moving everything to Percipience wasn't a bad one, especially if they could send a team there.

Even with all the excitement, Lauren couldn't hold back a yawn. It was only a few hours to sunrise. Everyone agreed it best to try for a few hours' sleep. Jordan ordered four guards to watch over the pyramid's entrance. When she reached her tent, her thoughts were still at the marble wall and with her feelings for Alec. She rolled out her sleeping mat and lay down close to him, remembering how she had felt while they kissed. The discovery of WISE and the changes it would bring excited her, but her heart had never responded to anyone or anything as it had at that moment.

She was also surprised to feel afraid, an unfamiliar emotion for her. She knew her fear didn't stem from premonitions about the pyramid, but what would soon happen when he would leave and return to Epoch and to his close friend, Allison.

16 - RETURN TO EPOCH

To Jordan's relief, Jake was surprisingly supportive of having the crates moved from the pyramid to Percipience and setting up WISE there.

"I told Allison and Kimberly just the other day that our next focus for the Re-Discovery Center would be in electronics," he said. "We'll be able to make very quick progress with the help of the WISE system. Robert, are you sure you'll be able to handle the move to Percipience safely?"

"I'm going to call Percipience," Robert replied, "The plane parts should be ready by now, and I'm pretty sure that I can get enough manpower over here within the next day or so."

"That will work out well. Jordan, I want you and a few of your best men to help," Jake said. He knew it wasn't a perfect situation. However, in the end, it would not only be a good reason to complete the road to Percipience, but it would also put a team there to gather intelligence.

Robert made a quick radio call to Percipience, and the plane parts were indeed ready. He quickly went over the current situation and instructed them to get a few hundred able-bodied men and women up to Little Bear Lake with the parts as quickly as possible.

To everyone's surprise, the first group from Percipience arrived just before the evening meal. Travelling light, they made the trip in record time, and by sunset, the full contingent of two hundred had arrived.

Starting in the morning, this group, with Jordan and a few others from Epoch, sorted through the crates and started the journey back to Percipience. The rest of the Epoch team closed the pyramid door, sealed the entrance with rocks and went with Robert, Alec, and Lauren to see if the new plane parts worked.

"I sure hope that nothing in those crates gets damaged on the trip back," Alec said to Robert as they hiked down the hill to Big Bear Lake.

"Don't worry. They know the value of those crates are and will be extremely cautious. They'll be back in Percipience in less than a week. I'm just hoping the parts work so you won't have that long horseback ride to Epoch."

"Back to Epoch?" Alec said. "No—if we can't get the plane going, I'm going back to Percipience with you. I've got to see what's in all those crates."

Lauren smiled wistfully as she listened. She had begun the day feeling saddened knowing that this was the day he would leave her.

They got to the plane in the early afternoon, and Robert showed Alec the repaired parts. "They were able to repair the timing chain," he said, "but didn't have much luck with the cylinder head, so they tried to make a new one. Hopefully, it'll do at least until you get back to Epoch." He knew that the cylinder head built in Percipience was superior to the original.

Alec focused on his current problems with the plane. He examined the chain and was unable to tell where the broken links had been. He looked over the cylinder head and was shocked at the quality of craftsmanship. He had made the original one and immediately saw that this had been built by someone with much greater skill. "Wow, this will more than do the job," he said. "How was it done?"

"They cast a mold of the old one and then worked the casting with some hand tools," Robert replied, lying in part. Numerous machines in a fully equipped shop had been used to complete the cylinder head. He had instructed the workers to make it functional, but they spent additional time perfecting the finish, making sure that the edges and corners were perfectly beveled and rounded.

It took Alec little time to restore the engine, and with Lauren and Robert watching from the lakeside, he entered the cabin and pressed the starter button and revved the engine a few times before shutting it down. Emerging from the cockpit, he shouted, "Perfect!" and raised his arms into the air.

Lauren had her hands over her ears. "Loud enough!"

He laughed at her discomfort. "And pure music to my ears," he said. "The oil pressure is a little low, but good enough for the trip back."

"You still leaving today?" Robert asked. "The sun is getting close to setting, and I thought you were planning on going to Percipience."

"No, I'm not taking any chances. I'll head out first thing in the morning, and since it'll take a week or so to get the crates to Percipience, I'll go to Epoch first and then fly up to Percipience when the crates get there."

He felt reluctant to leave and justified his reasoning with the practicality of safety concerns. Though they were technically far behind Epoch, he found the way of life in Percipience surprisingly appealing to him. The discovery at the pyramid and his growing attraction to Lauren made his return trip less desirable each day.

They camped by the plane for the night and discussed the following day's plans. "I have an idea," Alec said hesitantly to Robert. "I've been wondering if Lauren, and perhaps you, would like to make the trip back with me."

"In *that*?" Lauren said, pointing to the plane.

Robert's interest was piqued. "That's not a bad idea, Alec . . . "

"Are you serious, Dad?" Lauren interrupted, her voice filled with horror. "That thing crashed, and you want me to get into it and fly?"

"Lauren, I trust Alec. If he says it's safe, don't you think it would be wonderful for us to see his city?" Alec had already told them some about Epoch, and Robert needed as much information about the city as he could get—their technology and the character of their leaders. He had also grown to like Alec over the last month and found him to have a kind nature. The increasing attraction between Lauren and him was obvious.

"But what about the pyramid and the crates?" she protested. "I could stay behind and make sure that everything gets safely back to Percipience."

"Jordan will take care of that. It'll take at least a week or so before everything gets to Percipience, and by then, Alec will have flown us back, isn't that right?".

"Yes, of course," Alec quickly replied. He was happy to see that Robert was open to the idea.

"Then it's settled—in the morning, we'll go to Epoch."

Lauren knew the decision had been made and that her protests were useless. She would go along only because her father had decided on the trip.

The next morning, the last few members of the Epoch squad began their return to Epoch on horseback. Alec, Lauren, and Robert packed up their campsite and got into the plane. Alec was excited to be flying again and ran through the pre-flight checkout. He started the engine and with practiced skill guided the plane across the lake and into the sky.

Lauren clung to her seat as the plane cleared the trees. She gazed transfixed at the aerial view of the white pyramid when Alec passed over Little Bear Lake.

"Come in, Epoch, this is Alec." She listened as he waited for an answer.

There was a short pause before a voice was heard. "Hey, Alec! Great to hear from you! Is that a plane engine in the background?"

"It sure is, and it's purring like a kitten. Please tell my folks that I'll be arriving in less than two hours and that I have two guests with me from Percipience, Robert, and Lauren."

"Will do, Alec. See you soon!"

He decided against showing Coppertown to his passengers and flew straight to Epoch. As they got nearer, Lauren noticed a large section of land without trees. "Do you know what happened there?" she asked.

"That's part of our lumber mill operation," he said. "We clear-cut the trees, using the big ones for lumber and the smaller ones for pulp. It's more efficient this way, and we do plant trees after the clearing. If you look on the other side of the plane, you can see a section similarly treated about twenty years ago, and it looks like the original forest now."

She looked out the other side of the plane to a section of unhealthy looking forest land. The trees stood in straight lines, and there was little other plant life. *It's not the same at all.*

A short distance later, Alec proudly pointed out the coal-mining operation. This land had also been stripped to accommodate a surface mine for gathering coal. From here, the coal was placed on a barge that made its way to Epoch. She thought of the scale of plant and animal life displaced, and the long-term damage caused, all for coal, which would, itself, harm the environment.

Skater Lake soon appeared, and Alec passed over some of the farm land near Epoch. "Are those cows?" she asked. She had never seen one outside the pages of a book before now.

Her enthusiasm delighted him. "Yes," he said. "And there are some sheep as well down there. The smaller, white, puffy creatures."

They began to descend, and the plane glided smoothly toward the lake. Despite the excitement of their unprecedented adventure, Robert and Lauren felt relieved to feel their feet on the earth again and grateful for an uneventful landing. News of Alec's return had spread through Epoch. A large crowd had gathered on the shore as the plane floated towards the town. He pulled up along the dock and saw his parents waving at him.

He stepped out of the plane as Kimberly and Allison arrived at the dock. Allison could think of nothing but holding him as she ran to greet him. Her eyes were drawn to the girl standing in the exit doorway. She was tall, beautiful, slender, with long, blonde hair and doe-like eyes. She was nearly Alec's height and at least half a foot taller than Allison. *This must be Lauren. No wonder it took Alec so long to get back.* She tried not to show her jealousy as she reached Alec and gave him a big hug, which he reciprocated.

"I missed you so much, my love," she said loud enough for everyone to hear. She pulled him toward her for a lingering kiss.

At that moment, Lauren witnessed her worst fears come true. Jealousy and anger were overshadowed by the sadness she felt cutting into her.

Robert could feel his own anger as he thought of how Alec had obviously led his daughter on. The dock suddenly swayed, jolting Robert and Lauren back into the moment.

17 - REALIZATION

Robert was the last person to leave the plane, and Jake was shocked at the size of the man. He had heard from Jordan that the men from Percipience were big but was not prepared for this bear of a man standing to his full height. *He must be at least a foot taller than I am—and he looks awfully strong.*

When Alec had made the introductions, Jake stepped forward. "Robert, I would like you to be my guest while you're in Epoch. I have also arranged for Kimberly and her parents to host your lovely daughter."

"Come along, Lauren," said Kimberly, "let's get you settled at my place and then we can take you on a tour. Are the rest of your things in the plane?"

"Things?" replied Lauren, still shaken by what she had seen between Alec and Lauren. "This is all I have." She pointed to her backpack. "We came here right from the pyramid."

"Oh! You must tell us everything. Your discovery has been the talk of the town. Don't worry about not having your stuff. You're a little taller, but otherwise we're the same size, and you can borrow anything that you need."

She followed behind Kimberly and was thankful that Allison had whisked Alec away. The newness, and especially the size of her surroundings, despite all that Alec had told her, was unexpectedly shocking.to her. She was fascinated by her first tram ride and was amazed to see so many people and buildings all in one place.

Kimberly's mother was thrilled with their celebrity visitor and showed her to the guest bedroom, which she pronounced would be Lauren's for as long as she was in Epoch. Lauren remembered her discussion with Alec about sleeping arrangements, but now that she saw it for herself, she began to understand why her way of life in Percipience seemed so strange for him. She viewed the large room as a waste of space especially knowing she was its only occupant.

After a cup of tea and ceaseless questions, Kimberly rescued Lauren and fitted her with some of her own clothes. She accompanied her on a quick tour of the town before supper, starting with the warehouse.

There were the usual armed guards from the DC at the entrance when they arrived, and a line of people waiting to get their ration slips filled. Kimberly explained that the warehouse was no longer only for scavenged items from before the Great Loss, but also for critical items that included specific foods and medicines that were in short supply.

"Of course, you can buy most of these things in the private store if you don't have a ration slip, but the prices are higher," Kimberly said.

Lauren didn't understand but decided to not ask. Instead, she tried to take in all the new sights. As they walked up the hill to see the other shops, they passed a street vendor selling leather purses. She couldn't help noticing the uneven stitching and poor quality. Kimberly was attracted to two of them.

"Aren't they beautiful?" she said as she stroked the leather and admired the exterior design. "I so wish I could have one, but I don't know which one to pick."

Lauren saw the sign above a pair of dice that lay on the stand: "Roll a twelve and your purchase is FREE!"

She pointed to the sign, and Kimberly smiled. "He's been selling things for years and claims that some people win, yet I've never heard of anyone who has. My guess is that the dice are weighted so that a twelve will never show up."

The vendor, a heavyset man, saw Kimberly's interest and gave her a sales pitch on the high-fashion style and durability of the purses.

"I really like them but just can't afford them today," she said and turned to leave.

"Wait!" Lauren said. "I don't understand this money thing very well, but do you have enough for one purse?"

Kimberly pulled out all her money, enough to buy one. "But we can't spend all of this—I need it to buy food and things, and I don't get paid again until next week."

Lauren barely heard her as she took the money and looked at the vendor. "I'll take this one," she said, holding up the purse that Kimberly had been looking at. She put the money on the vendor's cart.

"A fine purchase!" He scooped up the money with practiced skill, but with surprising strength, Lauren swiftly grabbed his wrist.

"Not so fast," she said, "I get to roll the dice, don't I?"

Startled by her quick movement, he stood back. "Of course," he said, trying to sound convincing. "I was just about to give them to you"

He handed her the dice, and she knew immediately that Kimberly had been right. She gave them an exaggerated shake, threw them onto the cart, and watched as they bounced a few times. Each showed a six. Kimberly shrieked, and other shoppers stared in disbelief.

The vendor blinked as he stared at the dice. There was no time to recover.

"How about one more time?" Lauren asked, pointing to the money that he still held.

"Uhh . . . of course."

She picked up the dice again. Still looking at the vendor, she shook them twice before throwing them. She didn't wait until they stopped and took the money out of his hand. Kimberly and the crowd now gathered cheered when the dice once again stopped at double sixes.

Lauren picked up the two purses and handed them to Kimberly with her money.

"How did you do that?

"I had a feeling about it." Lauren replied as she continued up the hill. Kimberly ran to catch up, clutching her new possessions.

The rest of their tour was uneventful, and they arrived at Kimberly's house in time for the evening meal. Even with all of Kimberly's family in attendance, it seemed like a small gathering for Lauren, more used to having at least forty people around the table. She explained how, in Percipience, several families lived in the same hut, including children, grandparents, and great-grandparents.

"Great-grandparents?" Kimberly's father asked.

"Yes, my great-granddad died a few years ago, but my great grandma is still going strong. She's going to be 93 in a few months."

"I don't know if we have anyone that old here. Do we, Dad?" Kimberly asked.

"No, I think the oldest person in your grandpa's retirement home is around 80," he replied. Lauren had heard of retirement homes from Alec and had thought it was a silly idea for elderly relatives to live away from their families.

Before they began eating, Kimberly's father recited a grace, and the serving bowls were shared around the table. Lauren recognized most of the food except for a large platter of meat in the center.

"Cow?" she asked, pointing to the plate.

Kimberly and her younger brother giggled. "Right animal," she said, "wrong word. We call the meat we get from cattle, beef."

“I see.” Lauren explained that the only red meat available in Percipience was the occasional deer or bison. Once a week, they also might have a serving of synthetic meat. "I wonder if the extra fat and L-carnitine in red meat is one of the reasons for the lower age here," she remarked.

Kimberly stopped eating and looked at her. She had originally thought of Lauren, and, in general, the people in Percipience, to be somewhat uneducated based on the conversations had with Alec and Jordan. She asked how she knew about food content. Lauren described her father’s expertise in biology and chemistry and said that she found it fascinating and had spent as much time as possible in the lab with him.

After dinner, with the dishes cleaned, Kimberly and Lauren chatted in the living room. Lauren asked about a large box-like piece of furniture near a wall.

"Oh, that’s a record-player, back from before the Great Loss."

"I’ve read about them, but I’ve never seen one before. Does it still work?"

"There are not too many in Epoch, but yes, it still works. Let me put a record on for you." Kimberly got up and pulled a large, black disc from its cover and gently positioned it on the machine.

Lauren waited in eager anticipation. Two speakers released the sound of an orchestra playing the music of Mozart. As she listened, tears rolled down her face. "It’s so beautiful," she said. “I’ve heard this played on the piano before. Hearing it with a full orchestra is a hundred times better.” They listened together until the last notes faded into the evening.

When she climbed into bed, Lauren’s mind was spinning with all the day’s events, but her thoughts always ended with the image of Allison kissing Alec at the plane. A mixture of sadness, rage, and jealousy swirled through her. She replayed the scene, and for the second time that evening, she wept. Not like the soft tears when she had heard Mozart, but uncontrollable sobs that shook her until she fell asleep.

During the next week, with Kimberly as tour guide, Lauren tried to forget Alec and went to see all the sights of Epoch, including the Re-Discovery Center, factories, farms, and the greenhouse. They took a boat ride up the river to visit the lumber mill and the coal mine, neither of which impressed her. She realized this coal was probably the source of the mercury contamination that she had detected in the creeks near Percipience.

They ran into Clyde on several occasions, and although Kimberly tried to avoid him, apologizing for his animatedly odd behavior and ideas, Lauren took a keen interest and asked if he would have lunch with them sometime. He accepted but insisted they meet at his house, and he gave them directions to the outskirts of town where he lived.

On the appointed day they were to meet Clyde, they took the tram to the stop nearest his house and discovered that there would still be a couple of miles to walk.

"Have you ever been to his place before?" Lauren asked as they walked along the path leading out of town.

"I don't even think I've been in this section of town before." Kimberly said. The area contrasted starkly with the neighborhood she had grown up in. Here, the homes looked more like a military base, no frills, all the same, and they seemed to go on forever. "I guess I'm lucky that my parents have good jobs. Most of the people who live here are laborers and don't make near the same amount of money."

"What's the story behind Clyde?" Lauren asked. "Why is he so different from the others in Epoch?"

"I don't know, really. He's a few years older than I am, and from what I've heard his mom and dad were the same way. Never wanted to be involved with the rest of the town or have any kind of steady work. There was an accident, though, a few years ago, and they were both killed. Clyde was their only child, and he's been taking care of himself ever since."

They reached the end of the row houses, and after another half-mile walk, they found a small path leading into the woods. True to Clyde's directions, the path curved up a hill, and from the top, they could see a house surrounded by trees in the valley below. Lauren laughed when she read the sign beside the path: "You are now leaving Epoch!"

They had no set expectations, but Clyde's home would have far exceeded any they might have had. His house was small, with two bedrooms, and looked like a structure built before the Great Loss. It was made from stone, and a new roof and porch had recently been completed. A large and meticulously kept garden had been landscaped around the house, and the property was bordered by a log fence of natural wood.

They looked at each other in surprise and approached the front porch. Clyde came out to greet them.

"Hey, right on time! Glad you could make it."

"This is quite a home and garden you have here," Lauren said, pointing to the neatly tended rows of vegetables.

"Yeah, it must be a pile of work to keep up," Kimberly added.

"Not nearly as much as I'd have to do to earn money and pay for food in the store," he said. He motioned for them to follow him behind the house and along a small trail that led deeper through the trees. They walked for a few minutes before the forest gave way to a small clearing. He stopped and waved his arms dramatically. "This is my second, secret, garden."

It was a small patch of land comprising marijuana plants, all at different stages of growth.

"Clyde, you know that this is so illegal, don't you?" Kimberly asked. She was amazed to see plants she knew only from pictures in books.

"That's what Alec said too." Lauren said. "But what's wrong with these plants? We grow acres of hemp and cannabis in Percipience."

"Acres?" Clyde said. He sounded incredulous.

"Yes, of course. We use it for clothes, paper and the like, and we smoke some too. It has a lot of medicinal qualities and is far better than other mind-bending stuff like liquor." She saw his smile widen, and his eyes become brighter.

"Finally, someone who understands!" and he began to show her the various strains that he was growing.

"So why is this illegal?" she asked again.

"It makes sense if you don't think about it too hard."

"Huh?"

"Sorry, I couldn't resist . . . "If it were legal, there'd be a lot less beer and pharmacy drugs sold, and the companies that produce them would make less money. At least, that's what I think is a big part of why it's illegal."

She made a funny face. "Yeah—I think you were right the first time. It does make sense if you don't think about it too hard."

She noticed that Kimberly looked uneasy being there, and she suggested that they all return to the house.

On the way back, Kimberly reproached Clyde. "I really don't understand why you smoke that stuff."

"Lots of reasons," he said. "Besides making life just a bit more pleasant, what I really like is how it plays with the senses. It helps to remove the filters that your brain puts up, and you start seeing things that have been blocked."

"Exactly!" said Lauren. "Deep meditation will do this as well, but marijuana will have the same effect, only not quite as controlled. My grandmother was one of the few people that I knew who understood this well, and when she explained it to me, I began to sense the same thing." She caught herself before saying much more.

Kimberly's interest had been piqued. "What kind of things do you see? And what kind of stuff can the mind block? We have five senses that we can hardly ignore."

She tried to explain without giving too much away about herself. "We're all born with abilities to sense far beyond the basic five senses—it's stronger in some people. For most people, if their minds can't understand what it's sensing, it will start to filter out information at an early age."

"How can your mind filter things out?"

"I'll try to explain it another way. Your mind will process only what it can comprehend. Without understanding, it'll either alter the sense to something that it *can* understand or block it out completely."

"Oh, like when you block out a memory because it's too painful to think about?"

"That's a good example. Have you ever heard about the upside-down glasses experiment?" she asked.

"Never."

"It's an experiment that was repeated many times before the Great Loss. People were asked to wear glasses that had special built-in mirrors that flipped everything upside down. After about three days, their brains flipped the image around so that now, things were right side up and made visual sense again. What's interesting is that when they took the glasses off, everything was upside down again for another three days until their brains sorted it all out again."

Kimberly saw that Clyde was listening as intently to Lauren as she had been. He walked closely behind between the two women.

"So when you think about it," Laura continued, "is it really so hard to believe that the mind will filter or block sensory signals until it can get to a comfortable enough place to comprehend what's going on?"

Kimberly still felt doubtful. "I don't know. I still have a hard time believing that there are more than the five senses."

"Okay," Lauren said, "without looking at your watch, what time is it?"

"Probably around 12:45," she said, glancing at her watch. It was 12:42.

"There, you have a sense of time passage as well," Lauren said, "There are several nonphysical senses, and depending on the person, they can be strong or weak."

Clyde felt like he had found a kindred spirit. "Wow! I've never met a person who actually understands this," he said. "Does everyone in Percipience think the same way?"

She turned and smiled at him. "No, not everyone, but they're much more open to it than people in Epoch appear to be. I think that Percipience residents attempt to understand their inner selves more, and relate that to their purpose in life, instead of just trying to get through life."

"What do you mean by purpose?" Kimberly asked.

"Well, let's say your purpose is equal to adding together values, strengths, passions, and services. If you strive to be true to these, then your life purpose is fulfilled. Most of this comes from Eastern religions that existed before the Great Loss," Lauren explained.

Kimberly nodded, but still did not understand all that Lauren had said.

Clyde, however, absorbed every word. "How far away is Percipience?" he asked. "Acres of weed and people who think so clearly . . . I've got to get up there!"

18 - RETURN TO PERCIPIENCE

It had been a week since their arrival in Epoch before Robert heard that the pyramid crates had arrived safely in Percipience. Looking forward to returning home, the news arrived none too soon for him. During the last week, he was given no time to himself, and he either Jake or a guard from the DC accompanied him wherever he went. Although polite, they obviously had discussed what he would see and areas and topics to avoid. *Can't blame them—I did the same thing to Alec.* Smiling to himself, he asked his current young guard to get word to his daughter that it was time to head home.

Robert and Jake had agreed that Kimberly would join them for the trip to Percipience, much to Allison's annoyance. Since Alec's return, he was rarely out of her sight. But she noticed changes in his demeanor; he seemed calmer and more reflective. She missed his more carefree and reckless attitude and hoped that the old Alec would soon return.

"Look, Allison, the plane was really only designed for four people maximum to begin with," he said. They stood by the dock waiting for Kimberly and Lauren to arrive. "It looks like Jordan will be up in Percipience for a while, so it makes sense to have Kimberly there. Besides, I'll be back in a few days."

She began to protest further when she noticed Kimberly and Lauren walking down to the dock. Then she realized that all eyes were on Lauren, dressed in an outfit of Kimberly's that fit her body snugly. She could have been mistaken for a high-fashion model as she gracefully approached her father and gave him a hug.

"Missed you!" she said.

"I missed you too. You certainly look different."

"Kimberly let me borrow some of her clothes while I was here so that I wouldn't stand out so much." Her smile evaporated when she saw Alec.

"Hi," he said. He knew that he would need to explain his relationship with Allison.

Robert could see the tension between them. "Are we all ready to go then?" he asked Alec.

"Yes, sir," Alec replied, glad for the diversion. "All fueled up and ready for takeoff." Alec had spent several days inspecting the plane's airworthiness. "I'm excited to get back to your village and open those crates!"

While the others talked, Allison took Kimberly aside. "I want you to keep a close eye on Alec," she said, "especially when he's around her," She pointed discreetly to Lauren.

"Sure, I can do that," Kimberly said, "But judging from how they're reacting to one another, I don't think you have much to worry about."

As the four walked down the dock, Lauren heard her name called and turned to see Clyde running to catch up with them. "Hi!" she said. "I'm glad you came to see us off."

She stopped when he reached them. "I wanted to say good-bye and to thank you and Kimberly for visiting me the other day. Our conversation was eye-opening for me, and somehow, I'm going to make it to your village as soon as I can."

"I enjoyed our visit too," Lauren said, "and I hope that you'll come to Percipience. But I'm sure that I'll be back here, so we'll see each other before too long," She smiled warmly and held his hand, mindful that Alec was watching her.

Lauren gave Clyde a quick hug and followed the others down the dock towards the plane. Before they boarded, Allison gave Alec a long good-bye kiss. "Come home soon," she said as he boarded and secured the cabin door.

He wasted no time getting into the pilot seat, and with a few flicks of switches, the engine roared to life and started the plane on its journey across the lake and into the sky.

He was glad to be back in the air and at the controls. While the others engaged in conversation, he could let his mind concentrate on his thoughts. He felt at a loss about his feelings for Allison and Lauren. *How could I have feelings for both when they're almost exact opposites of each other?* He thought about the cold response from Lauren, and that though it would be uncomfortable, he must find time within the next few days to talk to her about it.

It took a while for her to calm down after the show given by Allison. But as she did, she noticed that her father looked glum as well, which was unusual for him. "Is everything okay, Dad?"

Her voice brought him out of his own thoughts. "Yes, of course," he said. But she knew something was wrong and could sense that he was trying to keep something from her. With a small amount of effort, she could easily read further into his thoughts, but she respected him too much. To distract herself from wondering about Alec and her father, she looked out the window to try and enjoy the scenery as the plane headed north.

Robert remained lost in his thoughts. Even while closely monitored in Epoch, he had seen enough to worry him greatly. Between the fiat monetary system, central government control, and consumption-based behavior of the population, there was now no doubt that they were a serious threat to Percipience. He would have some very frank discussions with the other elders about the next steps that Percipience should take.

The plane passed over the highway building equipment where good progress was obvious on the road from Epoch to Coppertown. Kimberly was delighted. "Ah yes! It won't be long now before we'll have this road finished," she said to no one in particular.

Lauren, however, was not impressed by the large machines or the work being done but decided this was not the time to express her opinion.

To break up the tedium, Alec detoured over Coppertown to show the goal of the highway reconstruction project. Nearing their destination, he knew that something was wrong.

"What the hell!" he said as they got close to the dam that was near Coppertown, "When Allison and I flew over here a few months ago, the water level was well below the top of the dam. Now it's actually flowing over the top of it."

"Not just over it," Lauren said. "Look at that crack on the left side. The water is coming through it, and fast."

"That wasn't there before either," he said. "What happened?"

Robert had been looking the dam and sat back in his seat. "I know," he said, "Little Bear Lake drains into this, and with the rush of water from blowing the dam, I'm sure this structure couldn't handle the flow and sudden increase in pressure."

Alec radioed Epoch to let them know what he had seen, and soon Jake could be heard.

"Cracked? That's not good news at all."

Robert asked Alec for the mic. "Jake, if we had drained Little Bear slower, this probably wouldn't have happened."

"You don't know that," Jake replied.

"Regardless, this does put a cramp in your plans to get to Coppertown."

Jake asked Alec to do one more pass over the flooded dam to get a better assessment of the damage.

He circled the site while Jake waited. "We may be able to get light vehicles over it, but nothing heavy. The whole structure looks like it could give away at any time."

"We'll overcome this small obstacle," Jake said confidently before signing off but could offer no plans.

Coppertown appeared to look just as Alec remembered it. He pointed to some of the main features including the brick structure he believed had been a university, which keenly interested Robert.

"There could be many useful items in there, especially in the labs," he said, echoing Alec's thoughts at first sight of the structure.

Alec remembered his father's advice and thought that he might have been right. *Maybe we do need to push to get up here before Percipience gets the lab equipment and supplies now that they know it's all here."* He made a mental note to discuss this with Jordan and his father.

After Coppertown, they flew over the pyramid, which, at least for a few minutes, distracted everyone from their thoughts. They stared down the center of the emptied lake where the pyramid stood, its white marble and golden top looking as if it had just been built.

"Hard to believe something like this is here," Kimberly said. "We could find nothing on it at the Re-Discovery Center. You'd have thought that building it couldn't have gone unnoticed prior to the Great Loss."

"Well, some things can be hidden without even trying," Robert said, "After all, we've been living close to each other for over 200 years."

"I guess you're right," she replied. She recalled Jordan's suspicions about Percipience intentionally hiding from Epoch during that time. *If they were hiding, was all of Percipience in on it and Lauren's innocence all just an act?* Thoughts ran through her head as the plane banked away from the pyramid on its way to Percipience.

19 - NEGOTIATIONS

The plane made a couple of low passes over Percipience before landing at a small lake that was a mile from the village. By the time the plane was close to shore, a small crowd had gathered to see the flying machine.

Without a dock, securing the plane and getting onshore was a wet process. But Alec was happy to be back and to focus on something other than Lauren and Allison for a while. Jordan was one of the first people to reach the plane and was happily surprised to see Kimberly in the co-pilot's seat.

"Didn't expect to see you."

"Yeah, we thought we'd keep me as a little surprise for you," she said. She splashed into the knee-deep water and hugged him. The awkward feelings between Alec, Lauren, and Allison had made her appreciate her relationship with Jordan.

When they all reached shore, they began their hike along a winding trail from the lake back to the village. Jordan suggested to Robert that they think about replacing the path with a straighter and wider one.

"Most of the traffic in Percipience is by foot, Jordan. This path is fairly direct and flows naturally between the trees. I don't see the need to change that."

Jordan said nothing as he adjusted Kimberly's backpack that he carried. He was unsure how long he would stay in Percipience but could already see that Robert would not be easy to sway.

When they arrived at Percipience, Alec noticed a new, small, log building near the Research Center. Robert explained that while the crates were being brought from the pyramid, he had asked others from Percipience to construct this building so that they could have a quiet place to work. He did not add that he preferred no one from Epoch looking around in the

Research Center, which would have been the only other place where they could have set up WISE.

Entering the new building, they found the boxes stacked up against one wall and several empty tables and chairs waiting to be used. They started examining the engraved plates taken from the pyramid with the crates.

"I've reviewed the sheets that came with the crates," Jordan said. "This one tells us about the type and amount of power that will be required. Robert, can you arrange to get that brought in here?"

"That shouldn't be too much of a problem." Robert made a mental note that they would have to build up a few more windmills and another water tank backup to power the system. He wanted to avoid these issues from being the excuse for Epoch to take WISE to their town. "I'll work on getting that put together and getting a dedicated feed running into here," he said.

Jordan scanned through the next several sheets. "It seems like there are a few different jobs here. It says that crates number eleven and up contain data discs with modular shelves. I think we can split up the work with some of us uncrating the discs and the others working on putting the computer itself together. Also, containers six through ten are showing as spare parts, so we should be able to stack those away for right now."

"Kimberly and I'll start with the data discs," Lauren said.

Alec and Jordan began to look for the spare part kits to get them separated and put away. Lauren found crate number eleven, broke the seal, and opened it. Inside, there were three stackable cases that held hundreds of discs, and each one had a label with a number on it. She did quick mental calculations. "Wow, Jordan, if all of the crates are packed this way, there would be over 20,000 discs here. That's a pile of information!" She started to plan the best way to stack the discs in the room.

"We could put them against these three walls; then we could put the tables in the middle of the room," Alec said.

Lauren disagreed. "No, I think we'll put the tables by this wall, next to the window."

He could see that she was still upset and would have probably disagreed with whatever he suggested. "Okay, that sounds fine," he said as he and Jordan put the spare crates aside and began to open other boxes.

After they had unpacked boxes and assembled the computers, they all stood back to admire their work. On the table were two work areas with screens, keyboards, mice, and disc readers, all of which were connected to the computers that sat on their own tables behind the workstations. Robert had an easy time bringing in the power. To his surprise, the founders of Percipience, for some reason, had put in an underground power line to the location of the computer hut. He had no idea why this had been done, but he took advantage of the saved time to hook up ceiling lights and Epoch's radio transmitter he assumed would get heavy use.

"Are we ready?" Lauren asked.

"As far as I can tell—what do you think, Alec?"

"I think we've triple checked everything, so let's give it a go." He stepped forward and hit the single power switch that everything was connected to. Immediately, a hum was heard, and a few lights began to flicker on the devices. No one dared breathe as the lights continued their dance. A loud beep came from the contraption in front of them. Words scrolled rapidly on one of the monitors and then a simple screen appeared on each.

They cheered at the sight of the working system then exchanged handshakes and hugs. Lauren read the text that showed on a monitor: "Enter disc 00001 in drive and press the return key," she recited. "It looks like there are instructions in different languages."

Laruen turned to get the disc and ran into Alec who had turned at the same time. He bowed gallantly to led her proceed and was rewarded with a scowl as she reached for the disc.

She handed it to Jordan. "This must be an important one. There are four discs labeled 00001, and I didn't see any others duplicated when Kimberly and I unpacked them."

He took the disc out of its case and put it in the reader. After scanning the keyboard, he found and pressed the key labeled "Return." The reader made a whirring noise, and the screen was replaced with another image, which had a single input field labeled "Enter Search Terms" and a few buttons, one labeled "Search," another marked "Browse," and the last one "Help." There were other buttons in different languages, their collective guess being that they all pointed to the "Help" page in the associated language.

"Help" was voted the first action, and after a short period of trial and error, they managed to figure out that they needed the mouse to activate the command. Jordan clicked on it, and the screen was replaced with a video of an older gentleman who spoke in a low, warm tone.

"It has sound!" Robert shouted and was brusquely quieted by Lauren as she tried to hear the words spoken.

".... and if you're watching this, then you must have gotten through these challenges. If you need a refresher class in English, press the button below at any time." A button began to flash on the bottom of the screen with its label cycling through many languages.

The voice continued.

"There are two ways to use this system. You can press the "Browse" button, and you will be presented with a series of topics you can select and read through. The other way is to type in any combination of words that describe what you're looking for, and then press "Search." The screen will prompt you if it wants another disc to show the information you're looking for. I realize there are much faster technologies out there, and hopefully, you will be able to construct them with this information library. The reason for building WISE in this way was longevity and ease of repair. If you don't take a hammer to these specially made discs, or pour a bucket of water on the computer, this system should last for a *very* long time. Happy learning!"

The video and sound stopped, and the original screen came back on the monitor.

"Okay, so what should we start with?" Jordan asked.

"I know just the thing to test this contraption," Alec said and pulled up a chair in front of the keyboard. He finally managed to type in "gas-engine valve spring alloy composition," and with a show of flare clicked on the "Search" button. The screen changed and showed him a list of twenty articles and a brief description of each. He clicked on the first and was instructed to enter a disc. With the appropriate disc inserted into the reader, the screen changed to show a long article outlining the purpose of valves and springs in a gas engine and a range of alloy compositions for each.

Alec and Jordan were ecstatic. "Do you know how fast we'll be able to build things now?" Jordan exclaimed.

"My turn!" Lauren said, and after many keys had been pressed, she was rewarded with music and video of a concert hall. An orchestra played a Mozart piece. "This is the same music I heard on a record player in Epoch last week," she said.

All sense of time was lost. They took turns searching for random subjects, and it was nearly dark when a young boy came to the room to remind them it was supper time.

"I can see that we'll have to put a clock in here," Robert commented.

Jordan reluctantly clicked the power-down button as he had learned to do from the instructions, and they all left for Lauren's hut and the evening meal.

Alec was familiar with the Percipience routine, but it was new to Jordan and Kimberly. To Robert's surprise, Alec took over the teaching role, explaining the differences and pointing out several advantages to the way things were in Percipience.

“With their culture and lifestyle, look at how few resources they need, and how little labor it takes," he said.

“But what about personal belongings, clothes, furniture, and other stuff that’s needed?” Kimberly asked.

“Most of that, if you really think about it, isn’t needed. Back in Epoch, we already have so much stuff that we use only occasionally.”

Jordan listened to the exchange and recognized how much Alec had changed. *I wonder what side he would choose if it came down to it?*

After the meal, everyone in Lauren’s hut gathered around the fire pit and listened to Robert explain the computer setup and reference searches. There were lots of questions and even more suggestions for new subjects to look up. It was soon apparent that a system would have to be created to allow everyone a chance to use the machine.

As the night wore on, the rest of the clan returned to the hut to sleep. Jordan, Alec, Kimberly and Robert stayed up to discuss how to divide computer time.

"There are two terminals,” Jordan said, “so are we going to have one for Epoch and one for you, or should we base it on population?"

Robert was surprised by the boldness of Jordan's statement and felt convinced that he had been carefully coached by Jake to make sure Epoch would be guaranteed a good share of computer time.

"I’m not sure of the best way to do it,” he said. “Basing it on population wouldn’t give Percipience much time since Epoch is at least five times bigger.”

"But we also have a large group of people dedicated to just this kind of activity," Jordan said. "They're rediscovering technologies from before the Great Loss. Of course, anything we discover, and what we've already re-invented, would be shared with you."

Alec was also surprised by Jordan's directness. His father had told him to watch out for Epoch's interests but had obviously spent more time with Jordan on this subject. His words were exactly what Jake would say.

Robert knew that he had little negotiating room here. The free technology offered by Jordan was essentially useless. Percipience had most of what its people needed, but he intended to hide that fact from Jordan and Alec for as long as he could. His computer interest was more in the non-manufacturing areas such as biology, chemistry, and how it could advance Percipience in arts and literature.

"How about splitting it down the middle? Epoch can have full use of one of the terminals, and with the other, we'll split the time 50/50." Robert said.

Jordan considered the possibility. "Yes, that seems fair, at least for now. We can see how it goes. Alec, let's have a quick radio chat with your dad before we turn in."

Alec looked at Robert for approval, and when he saw him nod, agreed to the discussion. Kimberly followed Alec and Jordan into the darkness towards the computer hut, and Robert went to meet with the elders. He felt pleased with the way things were going, though at a quicker pace than anticipated and knew that they would have to accelerate their own plans. As he walked, he remembered to turn on a special portable radio hidden in his jacket. The receiver automatically synched to whatever frequency the radio in the computer hut was tuned. He was sure that it would come in handy in the weeks to come.

20 - FIRST SETTLEMENTS

Although he knew the path, Alec was glad there was moonlight to guide them to the computer hut. Other than crickets, and the occasional bird, it was very quiet even when they passed other clan huts. This was in sharp contrast to Epoch, where there was activity every hour of the day.

When they got to the hut, they powered up the radio and dialed in the new frequency that Jake had given them for private communications. Within a few minutes, they were in conversation with him, and Alec apologized for the late hour.

"No problem," Jake said. "I was here working through a stack of papers. How did your day go?"

Alec and Jordan filled him in on the day's activities including the assembling of the computer, the two terminals, the stacks of discs, and the searches they had done. They told him about the computer-usage deal that Jordan had struck with Robert.

"Excellent, excellent!" Jake was enthusiastic in his approval. "Very good work on the negotiations, Jordan. If we need more time, we'll just re-negotiate. Between you and Alec, I'd like some kind of schedule sorted out where we get the plane to do several flights back and forth over the next several days. I want to set up a camp of a dozen people or so to run our share of the computers around the clock. Bring this up with Robert to let him know that a team will be arriving. For now, they can live in tents, and as time permits, we'll build a more permanent structure up there."

"Okay, Dad," Alec replied. "One of us will fly out in the morning. And one other thing. We flew over Coppertown on the way up, and Robert showed a lot of interest in the old university grounds. I think he may send people there to see what they can salvage from the labs. Maybe we should get someone over there soon."

Jake was surprised by the information. "Yes, Alec, I certainly agree. We can drop off a few people on one of the trips up there."

"Can I be part of that?" Kimberly asked Jordan. "I feel like I've missed out on this entire discovery, and I have a good knowledge of lab equipment and supplies."

"Sure," Jordan said. "We'll set it up so that you and I can do this together sometime in the next couple of days." He turned back to the radio.

"Sir, Kimberly and I will head over to the University grounds in the next week."

"Good," said Jake. "I want both of you to keep a lookout for anything unusual. We want to make sure we're one step ahead of anything they may be planning. And the first member of the team you'll be bringing up there wants to say hi."

Allison's voice sounded cheerful and excited. "Hi, Alec!" She had been brooding about his being in Percipience with Lauren until Jake raised the idea of her spending some time there too. She jumped at the opportunity, and Jake was happy. He would have one more person that he could trust on site.

Caught off guard, Alec knew this had been a last-minute decision, and he wasn't sure how he felt. He chatted with her briefly then pointed out that they all had a long day ahead of them tomorrow and persuaded her to sign off. He and Jordan turned off the radio and headed out to catch up with Kimberly.

Jordan and the other men from Epoch had been invited to stay in one of the clan huts, but he felt strange about sleeping with so many people in one room. He opted instead to set up a small camp near the newly constructed computer hut.

The morning, which came much too early for Jordan's liking, was full of surprises. They went to Lauren's hut, and Alec immediately went to the kitchen and returned with two mugs of steaming hot, black liquid. He offered one to Jordan. “Coffee," he said with a grin. “It grows on you quickly and will wake you up."

Jordan was surprised at how easy their talk with Robert was about setting up a permanent Epoch camp. He seemed agreeable not only to their request to setup the camp but also to their bringing in several more people. He even extended the idea.

"I’ll talk to Jake today and see if he’d object to a few people from our village spending a bit of time in Epoch and at your Re-Discovery Center."

Alec and Jordan agreed that this was a good idea, and after a quick meal with coffee refills, they went down to the computer hut.

Lauren was already there. "My Dad told me about the deal that was made for computer time." Her voice was tinged with annoyance. “I thought I’d better get time in now before the schedule is in place." Her monitor showed a picture of a map of Earth with a series of connecting lines. "A fascinating paper on Earth's energy grid, vortices, and pyramids," she answered to the unasked question. Neither Jordan nor Alec had any idea what she was talking about.

****

Usually, both would choose flying over anything else. They challenged one another to see who would pilot the plane, but with the introduction of the computer as an alternative, there was no real loser. It was Jordan who suggested that Alec takes the first flight to ferry the Epoch team to Percipience. Alec promised to return by afternoon with Allison and the others. Lauren stiffened at the mention of Allison's name but tried not to let it show. She had accepted that Alec was involved with her and that he likely hadn’t intended for things to progress with her as much as they had.

After Alec left, Robert and Jordan worked out a detailed schedule for computer sharing and scouted out a suitable, long-term location for the

Epoch team's campsite. They found a spot about a quarter of a mile from the computer hut and close to the river.

"This site will work well," Jordan said. "We can set up a few tents here and perhaps run a pipe in for some fresh water. What do you think?" he asked Kimberly, who had joined them.

"Sure, this will be fine," she said hesitantly. "How long will we be here?"

"It could be a while, probably a year at least."

"I think that could work," Robert added. "Some of you may be fine with living in a tent, but I also think that you may want to get some kind of permanent structure built. A year is a long time to be living in a tent. I can arrange for a few of my men to help you build a cabin here if you're interested."

Jordan saw Kimberly's eyes light up at the mention of a cabin. He also noticed Robert's nod and meaningful smile.

"I guess you're right," Jordan said. "I've only been thinking about working with the computers and not that we'd actually be living here. How long would it take to build?"

"That would depend," Robert said. "My guess is that that you won't want a hut like the ones we have. You're probably more interested in a large cabin with lots of rooms."

"And a kitchen and washrooms," Kimberly said. Her smile lit up her face.

"Of course!" Robert said to Kimberly. "How about this: when Allison gets here this afternoon, the two of you sit down and sketch a rough plan, and we'll figure out how long the construction would take. Meanwhile, I'll get a few men working now to start bringing in water and power to the site. The main lines aren't too far away, and that won't take them more than a few days."

Kimberly was thrilled at the idea of designing the cabin. "Alec and Allison should be back soon, so I'm going to get started right away."

"Thanks, Robert," Jordan said.

"Well, regardless of what you're doing, you have to enjoy the present. You would've been all right in tents, but this will make things much easier for everyone. I can put a bunch of men on the project so I can't imagine that it'll take more than a few weeks to build what the girls will design, and I think they'll be much happier here."

"I can see that now," Jordan said. "Kimberly loved your offer, and I want to see her happy. I should've thought about that first."

"All of us get too focused occasionally and hopefully from that we learn what's critical and what's not. Let's head back to those computers and do some searches on how to build a real log cabin. We haven't ever made one before, and we need to at least look like we know what we're doing."

As they headed back to the computer hut, Robert's thoughts were focused and clear. *That worked out perfectly. The added work of the cabin design will buy me time that I need, and I can get extra wires into this new structure and install a few microphones to hear what they are up to.*

It took nearly a week for Alec to fly the entire Epoch team and their supplies up to Percipience. During this time, Jordan kept very busy setting up work schedules and details on how they would coordinate research time with Epoch. In what little spare time he had, he helped Kimberly and Allison, who were immersed in the cabin design and construction. They finally settled on a simple, but large structure, with a common area, kitchen, three bathrooms, and eight bedrooms, more than enough for the team since most were couples.

With Robert's construction crew beginning work on the cabin and the Epoch team settling into a routine of getting research requests from Epoch and using WISE to fulfill them, Jordan felt that things were going smoothly enough for him and Kimberly to visit the university grounds at Coppertown.

It was early in the morning when Kimberly got into the plane with Jordan. "This is going to be fun," she said as she hugged and kissed him before attaching her seatbelt.

'Yes, I'm looking forward to it too," he said. "It'll be nice to spend some time with you and get away from all this commotion."

"I was talking about exploring the university grounds," she said laughing, as he went through the pre-flight checklist. He guided the plane from the newly built dock, and within an hour from leaving Percipience, they had landed at the lake bordering Coppertown.

"It's hard to believe that we're walking through what used to be a town a few hundred years ago," she said. They went through an area that still had a few remaining structures.

"I know—and most of the houses, cars, and roads have been nearly completely reclaimed by nature."

They walked around what used to be the foundation of a house and started up the hill towards the university complex.

"There doesn't look like there's much salvageable stuff remaining here," she said.

"You'd be surprised. There are miles of copper wire underneath the ground that will be in perfect condition, and it'll be easy to get to with a little excavating. There'll also be lots of stuff still above ground. Let's take a look over here." He left their path for an area that could have been a house at one time.

With Kimberly behind him, he dug around for a few minutes. "Here we go!" He pulled a plastic tub away from the fierce grip of a few shrubs and carried it back to the path and opened it up.

“Christmas ornaments!” she said.

He grabbed a handful of tinsel and scattered it over Kimberly’s hair. “This isn’t a good example, but there’ll be lots of things still above ground that we’ll be able to use."

“I get it." She pulled at the last bits of trailing tinsel. Let’s see what we can find up there," she said, pointing towards the university.

When they reached the buildings, they were surprised by how good they still looked. Many of the windows were broken, but the brick structures had remained intact with even the roofs still in place in many areas. Jordan broke down one of the doors with little effort, and they began to wander through the halls.

He suddenly pointed and grabbed Kimberly’s arm.

“Hey!” she said, following his gaze. Several very recent footprints were clearly visible in the dust on the floor. “Who? . . . ”

Jordan put his fingers to his lips. They stood motionless for several minutes listening for sounds.

“I think whoever was here is gone now,” he said softly, “and now that I’m looking more closely, I can see footprints going in both directions."

They made their way through the halls, waiting to hear any kind of sound. The footprints showed entries into the doorways of laboratories, classrooms, and offices, but then turned and exited without further investigation.

“They were obviously looking for something very particular," Kimberly said. When they reached the chemistry wing, the number of footprints increased and showed entry into the department’s storeroom for chemicals.

"Judging by the number of footprints coming and going here, it looks like this is what they came for," Jordan said. He pointed to an emptied section of shelves. "They had no interest in the equipment just whatever chemicals were on these shelves."

"I wonder who *they* are, and what was on those shelves," Kimberly said nervously. "Let's get out of here. This place is giving me the creeps. We can tell Jake what we've seen and let him decide what to do."

Jordan agreed, and they quickly backtracked to the plane.

****

"Just chemical supplies? No equipment?" Jake asked after hearing their report on the progress at Percipience and their visit to Coppertown.

"It appears so," Jordan said, "But why the secrecy? If Percipience needed something, Alec or I would've flown it there if they had just asked. It has to be Robert, doesn't it?"

"Probably, but we don't have proof, and I don't want to get Percipience upset with us by accusing them. But something is happening here. Don't mention any of this to anyone right now, but keep an eye open for other suspicious-looking activities."

They nodded their agreement and left Jake to return to Percipience.

Jake started to dig through another pile of papers, but his thoughts distracted him. *Did Robert come up with the plan to build that cabin in Percipience just to keep Kimberly and Jordan in there and to give himself time to get what he needed from Coppertown? I may have underestimated him.*

For the next week, Jordan's team in Percipience organized working the research requests coming in from Epoch. They were also excited about moving into the cabin scheduled to be completed within the following week. Everyone, except for Allison, was happy with these arrangements. She was thrilled being close to Alec, and with working with Kimberly as part of the team, but what she had thought would be like a vacation turned out to be much harder work than she had ever done in Epoch.

With Jake's full support, Jordan had been appointed leader of the Epoch camp. To make the most of their computer time, he laid out a schedule that had members of the Epoch team working fifty hours per week. In addition to regular work, team members were obliged to prepare food and keep their own camp running, all of which left little free time.

Allison also missed the shops, restaurants, and socializing with people in Epoch. The town of Percipience was beyond understanding for her and the others from the Epoch camp. They watched as people appeared to work only in the mornings then did whatever they wanted the rest of the day. When she brought this up with Alec, he nodded as if he understood.

"It's pretty simple, really. They have very few material possessions, and their town isn't growing. If we decided to leave Epoch the size that it is now, and if we didn't buy things for ourselves, we wouldn't have to work that hard either."

"But we *need* to expand," she said. "By expanding, we're able to make more of the things we want. Like your plane, for instance."

He grinned in agreement. "That's right if that's what they really want. But they have zero desire to own anything. It doesn't mean they don't advance or ever have new things, though. Everything here just happens at a much slower pace. Take Robert—he loves chemistry and biology and spends his free time working on experiments in his lab, some begun by his father years ago. Others have a passion for wood or metalworking, music, cooking, etc. By doing things they renjoy, they never really have a job or work as we understand it."

She shivered. "Well, I couldn't live like that for very long. Though I'll admit that I don't enjoy *this* very much." She waved her arms to include the computer, discs and radio. "But I do enjoy the things I can buy with the money I make." She turned in her chair and continued logging data requests.

The small group that had gone from Percipience to Epoch didn't have similar issues. Jake was thrilled at Robert's suggestion to send a team to Epoch. He had thought that by integrating them into the town, they would see its advantages and return to tell the others in Percipience. However, this is not at all what happened.

When the group arrived in Epoch, they politely refused Jake's offer for them to stay with local families. Instead, they set up a small camp on the outskirts of town near the lake and remained self-reliant from the day they arrived.

Each morning, they arose and spent half the day at the Re-Discovery Center, learning and helping where they could. They gathered food for a couple of hours, and the rest of the day was dedicated to the activities they enjoyed. These included games, practicing on musical instruments, various forms of art, which were mostly sculptures made from rock or wood. They presented popular musical shows regularly at the town center, and their art works, all in high demand, were given away.

No one seemed to mind at first, but soon local business owners voiced the shared complaint that on the nights when there were performances, their own businesses slowed considerably.

This behavior infuriated Jake, and he tried numerous ways to force the Percipience team to adopt Epoch's way of life. His first attempt was getting a law passed that made it illegal to camp on town land. The team responded by moving a mile away. He made it illegal to perform concerts without a license and paying the town a tax. Much to his chagrin, he found that the people of Epoch seemed quite willing to visit the Percipience camp to listen to the free music. The evenings had become more popular than ever.

Eventually, Jake gave up and agreed that the Percipience team should move back to Epoch. They thanked him for the offer and said they were content where they were and asked if he would mind their setting up a permanent camp there.

This was the final straw for Jake. He decided to make a trip to their camp and see firsthand what was going on. His drive to the outskirts of town was uneventful with only a few new scratches on his truck. He parked on the side of the road and walked along a well-worn path leading to a hill. When he arrived at the top, he saw a sign: "Now leaving Epoch!" Ten feet ahead, another sign read "Now entering Clyde Ville."

I should've known that he was behind this! he thought as he followed the trail down the hill. Expecting a camp of no more than twenty people, he was astounded to see at least a hundred people within eyesight. Some played or were listening to music, others worked in a large garden area, and still others went in and out of Clyde's house. A group of people were gathered in a circle around a fire pit.

"Clyde! What is going on here?"

"Hi, Mr. J," said Clyde. "Pull up a log and join us."

"I don't want to join you! What are you doing? Where did all of these people come from, and why are some of them working here? The city isn't going to pay them!"

The group laughed softly at Jake's warning, which further enraged him.

"Hold on, Mr. J. Nobody is working here, and they don't expect to get paid. Everyone puts in a few hours a day to tend to the garden, that's all. As for me, I'm teaching my new Percipience friends the fine art of glass blowing." He gestured to his new pieces of art consisting of a flasks and pipes. "In return, they're going to show me a little about carving." He held up a stone carving of a bear. "You're more than welcome to stay for a while. Look around, and see how the other half can live."

"I don't have time for this, Clyde." Jake had already seen enough. "Have fun while you can," he said and turned away to leave as quickly as he could.

During his return to Epoch, he thought it best to forget about Clyde and the Percipience team for now. He was too busy dealing with the rest of Epoch, the DC, and the highway to worry about anything else. He slammed his foot down on the gas pedal, and the truck lunged forward. *When the highway is finished, I'll fix this Clyde problem once and for all.*

21 - UNEXPECTED MYSTERY

The day started innocently enough. Alec waited for Allison to get to the plane for their flight to Epoch. They were to deliver a stack of hand-scribed notes from several days of computer research and return later in the afternoon with supplies and items that Allison insisted were needed for their new cabin.

He thumbed through the notes on the construction of the stone data discs and other computer equipment that his father had requested. His brain clicked on something he read.

"... This binary data is stored on a circular platter of marble, the same material that was used to build the walls and floors of the pyramid but polished to a high degree and etched with microscopic tracks using a laser beam…"

Must be a transcription error. He picked up the radio and called Jordan who was in the computer room working the day shift.

"Hey, could you check this reference?" He quoted the disc, article name, and page number.

"Sure—any particular reason why?"

"Probably nothing," Alec said, "but I think we should stress to everyone here how important it is to accurately transcribe stuff." He saw Allison walking down the hill towards the plane. "Anyhow, looks like I'm ready to go—see you this afternoon."

He saw what had taken Allison so long. She had transformed her appearance with expertly applied makeup to her face and eyes and bright red lipstick to her mouth. Her thick, dark hair had been brushed until it gleamed, and she looked attractively trim in a black sweater and black jeans.

"Wow, you look fantastic!"

"I did it all for you." She leaned over and kissed him, leaving him breathless. "Now, let's get this thing going, I'm dying to do some shopping in Epoch!" She buckled her seat belt and adjusted her hair.

Alec had never seen Allison look so beautiful, and he could only nod as he started the engine and coached the plane across the lake and into the sky towards home.

It was mid-morning when Lauren appeared in the computer hut to see how things were going. She hoped that Alec would be working today and was disappointed that Jordan was manning Epoch's terminal with Kimberly on the radio.

"Hi," she said, looking around. "Alec isn't working today?"

"No," Jordan replied, "he flew out an hour ago to deliver the transcripts to Epoch. He said he'd be back this afternoon and asked me to dig up a page in an article for him."

"What kind of article?"

He gave her a handwritten paper copy. "I just finished it—something on making computer-storage devices."

Lauren read the page and stopped. "Can you pull up this page again?" she asked Jordan.

He slipped the disc into the reader, clicked several keys, and with theatrical arm movements, invited her to read the page.

She looked at the screen briefly. "Kimberly, get Alec on the radio." Her voice was full of excitement.

"Why, what's so important?" Jordan started to ask.

"NOW!" Lauren said in a sterner voice than she had intended. "Sorry. I'll explain later, but we need to get in touch with Alec right away."

"Do you think it could be a typo?" she asked as soon as she heard his voice.

"You see it too? It could be a typo, but if it isn't, how did we miss it?"

Jordan jumped into the conversation. "Miss what? Would someone please explain what's going on?"

Kimberly read the page quickly but found nothing unusual.

"The article says "floors," and there was only *one* floor in the pyramid," Lauren said. She pressed the radio microphone. "Alec, I'm going to leave here soon and will probably camp at Big Bear Lake tonight."

"Okay," he replied. "Allison and I are nearly at Epoch. We'll stick to our original plan and get back to Percipience later this afternoon. We can fly up to Big Bear tomorrow morning and then go out to the pyramid together."

"Great," Lauren said, "I'll meet you at Big Bear tomorrow morning then."

"Can't Alec fly you and me up there too?" Kimberly asked Jordan. She was happy to find any excuse to not work the mountain of research requests.

"I don't see why not," Jordan replied, "I can arrange for both of us to have the next few days off."

"All right. It's settled then," Lauren said. "It's probably a typo, but I've meant to go back up that way for a few weeks anyhow."

She was looking for time to herself, away from the commotion around the computer, new people, and construction. Most especially, she wanted time to visit with her wolf as she had not seen him for a while. She left the computer hut to prepare for her trip, but first stopped at the Research Center to let her father know her plans.

Robert was deep in concentration as he mixed several chemicals together and was startled to see Lauren.

"Hi, Dad," she said. "You're not going to believe what we found on the WISE today." She told him about the possibility of multiple floors in the pyramid and the plans she had made with the others to go there and investigate. She was surprised to see that he wasn't more excited.

"So what are you working on?" she asked. As she got closer to the lab bench, Robert immediately rose and came around the table, successfully blocking her view. He put his hand on her shoulder and gently guided her to the door.

"Just trying to sort out this lead cement," he said, "I'm trying to find some chemicals that will increase the length of time that it remains stable."

She noticed wooden crates on the floor, all showing a faded label stamp from the University of Coppertown.

"How did these get here?" she asked. "And what's inside them?" She slipped out from under her father's arm and moved towards the boxes.

"We got them a few days ago," he said. "I sent a team over to that university we spotted while flying up here to get chemical supplies. Don't tell anyone from Epoch. I didn't tell them we were doing it, and they may get upset if they find out."

"Well . . . okay." She opened the top box. There were only a couple of different chemicals that she could see, and they weren't the kind that were frequently used. "But why did they bring back *this*?" She held up a jar. "We can make this fairly easily, and we use so little that even one jar this size would last us years."

"Her father took the jar from her hand and closed the container. "I need more now," he said. "I'm afraid I have work that needs to get done. Keep in touch, and let me know if you find anything in the pyramid."

She was barely through the door when he closed it behind her, and to her surprise, she heard the lock click.

The excitement of a trip back to the pyramid allowed Lauren to put aside her father's strange behavior. Within an hour, she was on her way to Big Bear Lake.

22 - POWER

Lauren awoke the next morning to the tugging of her shirt and the feeling of several small soft paws. She laid very still and carefully opened one eye. Soon two small grey-blue eyes came into focus followed by a pink tongue.

The three wolf cubs were excited by the prospect of having a new playmate in their pack and happily jumped around beside her and crawled over her. She got up from a restful night while trying to give each one equal attention. She had arrived at Big Bear Lake right after sundown the day before and made her way up to her wolf's den. She spent the night nestled in with her friend and some pups just as she did when she was a child.

An hour after she awoke, she heard the plane approaching, said goodbye to her friends, and made her way back to the lake.

It was noon when they stood outside the pyramid, which appeared just as they had left it. They dropped their packs by the old campsite and made their way up to it. After removing the rocks from the entrance, they climbed the ramp. Jordan turned the crank by the door, and Alec opened it to reveal the near-empty room.

Jordan went to the map and played the message from Richard explaining the purpose of the pyramids and the computer. Everyone listened carefully. "No reference to another room," Alec commented.

For the next few hours, they examined the floor and walls and ran radiation meters, all without success.

"I don't think we missed anything in here," Jordan said. "We checked around for days outside too and didn't find anything else."

"I agree," said Kimberly as the artificial light started to dim. She headed towards the door. "I'll turn the crank again."

"Wait!" Alec shouted, "Let it go dark." They all stood where they were until they were left with only a narrow shaft of light.

"Close the door," Alec said to Kimberly.

The room still wasn't completely dark, and as her eyes adjusted, Laruen could see the faint glow of a luminescent arrow on the floor. It pointed to a tile near one of the walls.

"Let's get the light back on and see what's there," said Jordan.

Kimberly opened the door and turned the crank. The room brightened.

Alec was on his hands and knees looking at the floor where the arrow had pointed. "Ha!" he said, brushing away dust that covered a hole about an inch in diameter.

"What do we do now?" Jordan asked.

"It's not too deep," Alec said, "only around half an inch. Maybe it's a recessed button. Let's get something to push it down."

Jordan ran outside and returned with an appropriately sized twig. Alec placed one end in the hole and put all his weight on the other end by stepping on it and almost lost his balance as it moved down a few inches.

A tremor vibrated through the floor for several seconds and stopped as abruptly as it had started. Excitement and fear crossed their faces. Lauren and Alec spoke at the same time. "Another outside door!" They raced to the opposite side of the pyramid.

They discovered another set of marble tiles had fallen from the outside wall forming an entryway like the other side, except that instead of the ramp leading up into the pyramid, this one advanced downward.

They cheered and slapped each other on the back. Alec hugged Lauren hard, and Allison saw the way they looked at each other. She knew in that moment there was a shared understanding that she and Alec never had, but even her jealousy couldn't diminish her excitement at the most recent discovery.

Alec led the group down the ramp. As expected, there was another door and another crank. When the door was opened, the space revealed a smaller room than the one above it and contained the same kind of map and buttons. The difference here was that there was no desk and only one large crate.

The group entered the room and went directly to the map. Alec pressed the button marked "English," and Richard's now-familiar voice began to speak from the walls.

"Ah, I'm glad you solved this riddle of the cache. With events unfolding the way they are, I couldn't finish this project before I needed to close and submerge the pyramids. Though incomplete, the treasure on this floor is such that I believe with a bit of work you will be greatly rewarded. The large box in front of you contains a cold-fusion reactor prototype that my research team has been working on. You'll also find discs and engraved plates explaining how it works and theories on the final steps remaining. The prototype already generates power, but not enough to be really useful. The last tests generated only a few hundred kilowatts of power. I'm told that it should be generating about a few megawatts, and cleanly I might add, from metals that are in abundance and that you should be able to easily obtain. Good Luck!"

With that, the room became silent as each of them tried to absorb what they had heard.

"A few hundred kilowatts?" Lauren said. "That on its own is a quite a lot of power!"

Jordan responded with growing exhilaration. "We use more than that in Epoch, but if we can get a few of these built and increase their output, then we'd be set."

That box is far too big to fit in the plane," Alec said, "I wonder how heavy it actually is." He attempted to move it, and to his surprise, he could lift one side slightly off the floor.

"Much lighter than I expected, though still pretty heavy. I think a few people could carry this to Percipience."

"We should work on a plan to get this to Epoch rather than Percipience," Jordan corrected.

"What? Why Epoch? Percipience is much closer, and we can always build another for Epoch."

"Percipience doesn't need it, and Epoch does," Jordan said. He felt annoyed that Alec couldn't see the advantage that the device would offer to whoever possessed it if it did all that the recording said.

The others could feel the increasing tension.

"Okay, how do you propose that we get it to Epoch?" Alec asked, "It's too big for the plane, and we can't let it sit here until a road can be built."

Jordan felt flustered. He knew he couldn't challenge what Alec had said, but he also knew that Percipience shouldn't be allowed to have control of what would be virtually free energy. "Let's open the crate and see if we can box it into smaller pieces that would fit into the plane."

It was obvious that moving the contents by plane would not work. Inside the crate was a machine of considerably complexity, a small box of data discs, and the printed plates, just as had been advised. Jordan snatched the discs and plates. "Okay, we can bring it back to Percipience, but the Epoch team there will be the ones who work with these discs."

Alec looked at the contents of the crate. "Fine," he finally agreed. "Let's put the crate back together and get going. Can you also get me a piece of marble or something we can use as a hammer?"

Proud of his own quick thinking, Jordan left to search for a makeshift hammer. The others arranged pieces of the crate for reassembly. Alec surreptitiously picked up a small package in the bottom of the box and slid it into his backpack. Lauren noticed his sleight of hand, but he ignored her raised eyebrow as he moved other pieces of the crate.

The following day, Jordan flew to Epoch to give Jake an update on the find and with the hope of getting some guidance on how to proceed. He left Alec and the girls at the pyramid site to wait for a few people from Percipience to arrive to collect the large box containing the reactor. While they waited, Alec was able to spend a few minutes alone with Lauren, and he gave her the package he had found.

"Backup discs, I presume," she said to him.

"Of course," he said grinning. "It didn't seem fair for Epoch to be in control of a marvelous gift that should be for everyone. I don't know what's gotten into Jordan's head lately, but he sounds more and more like my father every day."

"He's just seeking his approval," Lauren replied. "I agree this should be shared, but I'll still be careful when I use them. Her eyes darted left and right to make sure they were still alone before she leaned over and kissed him. "For some reason, I can never stay mad at you."

"I never meant to hurt you," Alec replied

"I know—it just took me a while to realize it," she said.

****

The discs and plates sat on the center of Jake's desk after their discovery the day before. He had heard Jordan's report on the finding of the cold-fusion reactor on the second floor of the pyramid. He glanced at the discs then looked up at Jordan. "You've done an excellent job. I like the way that you think under pressure. Cold fusion?"

"Yes, sir!" Jordan said. "The recording claims that even though it's not complete, the prototype can generate a few hundred kilowatts of power already and in theory could generate a few megawatts, all essential for nothing and with no real pollution threat."

Jake walked over to the window and looked outside. "Jordan, I know this may seem a great advancement for us, but we need to look at the bigger picture."

"Bigger picture? I don't understand. Free energy will be great for everyone."

"Great for some—not so great for others. A significant portion of Epoch's economy is based on energy right now, and several prominent people own shares in the new refinery. Giving energy away could do more harm than good. For now, let's leave the discs here in Epoch so that nobody finishes the reactor. I need some time to figure out the best way to handle this. I want you to make sure that the news of this reactor stays in Percipience."

"Yes, sir," Jordan said and could see he was being dismissed.

He left Jake's office more confused than ever. Jake did seem proud of the way he had handled the situation, but why would he not want to build the reactor right away?

23 - CONSTRUCTION

The excitement in Percipience built up during the few days it took for the reactor to arrive. Getting it working would mean more mechanization, which, until now, had been avoided since there were no means for clean portable energy. Farming implements were in high demand, followed by boat engines, and additional power for the village. There had even been talk about building an airship, like a blimp.

“How are they coming along with the reactor?" Lauren asked her father one evening at the dinner table. It had been a week since it had reached Percipience.

“No success at all,” Robert replied. “There are lots of ideas on how to get it working, but no one wants to risk trying anything. Without any instructions, they’re afraid they may break it."

“That’s too bad,” she said. Since returning, she had not mentioned to anyone but her father that Alec had managed to get her a copy of the discs that outlined how the machine worked. Robert made deals with the elders in neighboring huts to borrow their computer time so that Lauren could read up on the device. With her knowledge of chemistry, she quickly absorbed the process and was happy to discover that though the device was complex to build, operating it did not seem too difficult.

“Perhaps you should look at it," Robert said, raising his voice slightly so that everyone around the table heard him.

“I guess I could. I’ll go over to the machine shop in the morning. Who knows, maybe I can sense something from it."

The following morning, Lauren arrived at the shop and saw the reactor sitting on a low platform in the middle of the room. A small group studied the tubes, valves, and wires in the vain hope of trying to reverse-engineer the device without taking it apart.

She walked up to the platform and circled slowly around the intricate machine, stopping occasionally to examine parts and doing her best to make it looked like she was in deep concentration. To add to her performance, she stopped at what looked like the main control panel, sat cross-legged in front of it, and closed her eyes.

Her actions caught the attention of the workers, and they stopped to form a small group behind her, whispering among themselves.

After half an hour, she opened her eyes and got up, bowed dramatically to the machine, and turned to face the group. "Are you all ready to get this working?" she asked. Without waiting for a response, she began itemizing a litany of tasks to be completed.

Robert had witnessed her performance and complimented her on the immediate results.

"Thank-you," she said. "Without telling them about the operation discs, I had to do something that was convincing. After all, life without a bit of mystery and magic would be boring."

Under Lauren's direction, there continued a flurry of activity over the next few days. A permanent platform was built for the reactor, breakers and cables were installed, and parts of the machine were adjusted and tested to see if it had survived an inactive state lasting two hundred years. A spare electrical generator was hooked up to the output shaft of the Stirling engine that came with the reactor. It was hoped that the unit would generate enough power for the Air-Chair electrical motors.

The next step was putting in the fuel stock that came with the unit and then to start the warm up cycle which would remove air from the reactor chamber and pressurize the hydrogen in the Sterling engine chambers. Lauren told everyone to take a break since it would take about a day for unit to be ready.

Throughout the day, word began to spread through Percipience that progress was being made on the reactor, and by late afternoon, the machine shop was full of people. Alec and Robert found a place by the door to watch the event. As the day progressed, a series of green lights appeared on the control panel, and finally, Lauren signaled that everything was ready. She went up to the control panel, and with everyone's eyes on her, flicked a series of switches.

The crowd fell silent as more lights lit up on the panel. The machine began to emit a low hum. She monitored the gauges on the panel while adjusting several dials and seemed satisfied with the results.

"Are we ready?" she asked. A collective nervous tension could be felt throughout the room, and the crowd stepped back. She threw the main breaker switch that connected the electrical output of the reactor to the Air-Chair system.

'It's working!" Alec yelled from the doorway. He pointed to the chairs outside that now were gliding quietly among the trees. The crowd raced out of the machine shop with Lauren following behind.

'This is great!" Alec said when she reached the doorway.

"I couldn't have done it without you." She gave him an affectionate hug. "With the discs, I think I pretty much know how to build another unit now. And once we're sure this unit will keep running, I'll get them to turn it off and take it apart to show how to build new ones."

"What about improving it?"

"It actually generates enough power for our needs. People are more interested in making it a bit smaller so that it is easily portable. Others will start researching how to make it more efficient, but on their schedule."

Jordan was furious at hearing the news of the functioning prototype. "How is that possible?" he asked Alec, who was working with him and Kimberly in the computer hut. "You saw that unit—it was complicated, and there is no way they should've been able to figure it out this quickly."

Alec shrugged. "You've never given them enough credit. They're just as educated as we are, if not more so."

"Alec is right," Kimberly said. "Lauren's knowledge of chemistry, for instance, is very broad."

"Do you recall that cylinder head they made for our plane?" Alec asked Jordan. "The craftsmanship in that was at least as good as the best made in Epoch."

"I still don't believe it. If they were really advanced, they wouldn't need to live the way that they do," Jordan replied.

Alec stopped working and looked at Jordan. "You still don't get it. They've made a conscious decision as a group that they want to live this way."

Jordan impatiently waved away Alec's words. "This still doesn't fix the problem we have now. They have a functioning reactor. We'll have to make sure that word doesn't get to Epoch. Your dad was very specific. I'm going to restrict trips to Epoch for a while to make sure that nobody down there finds out about this."

Kimberly and Alec looked at each other and rolled their eyes. "If you think that'll help," Alec said. "But word will get out sooner or later. You can't keep something as big as this a secret."

Over the next several weeks, Lauren and others from the machine shop made a second reactor, and when it proved to be as functional as the first unit, a celebration was arranged to have it unveiled in the new power plant built to house it.

Celebrations were not limited to Percipience. A mild winter allowed workers to complete the highway reconstruction project from Epoch to

Coppertown on schedule, although there was a problem with the roadway over the dam.

Recent flooding of Little Bear Lake had weakened the dam considerably. As the large highway construction machines crossed over it, a piece of the dam broke off into the lake taking one of the big trucks with it. The dam remained partly intact and able to retain water, but the roadway was impassable. Enough equipment had been moved to the other side to finish the road, but new traffic would now go via barge across the lake, and this limited the size of the vehicles that the salvage team could use.

Notwithstanding the setback, a sizeable crowd showed up for the ribbon-cutting ceremony in Epoch. Following many speeches, the first of several trucks lumbered down the road towards Coppertown carrying the salvage crew and their equipment.

Not everyone cheered, however. Robert was not pleased watching the vehicles head north. He had flown in that morning to meet with Jake. After he had heard that the construction had already begun on a road from Coppertown to Percipience, he wanted to stress one last time that Percipience was strongly against the highway extension. After the ceremony, he found Jake at his office.

“I don't understand why you’re continuing with this project when you know that my village is dead set against it."

“Listen Robert, I do understand your concerns, and I promise to take things slowly, but you should realize that the integration of our villages will make us both stronger. Think about the increased trade, sharing of knowledge, and expansion of territory. Look, we’ve already put plans together for a new satellite village right besides Percipience.” Jake said as he pointed to a map on one wall that showed the area around Percipience which included the new city plans.

Robert studied the map for a moment and shook his head. “We don't want to trade anything. We have everything that we need, and we have no desire to expand. Which leaves knowledge sharing. We’ve gone out of our way to share as much of our culture and computer time as we possibly can. We've even tried to get information here on the cold-fusion reactor but have been stonewalled by Jordan. Have you even started to build one yet?"

Jake ignored Robert's question and already had heard the other arguments several times over the last few months. "Robert, there is zero risk for you here. Epoch is taking the full cost of rebuilding this road, and we've already started the work. Once it's finished, you'll see the advantages. Now, unless you have something more to discuss, I have a very busy schedule and a pile of paperwork that needs my attention."

Robert stood up and towered over Jake. "You're making a mistake. Don't think that Epoch will get away without paying a steep price for this," he said. He turned abruptly and left the office.

Jake let go of the pen he had been holding tightly and exhaled with relief. This was the first time in a long while that he felt fear.

Robert had planned to meet Lauren for lunch at the greenhouse, and she had found a private area for them by the time he got there. She was excited and waiting to tell him about Clyde Ville and how some people from Epoch were converting to the Percipience way of life. But Robert was not listening; he was still thinking about his conversation with Jake and the few alternatives Percipience now had left to prevent Epoch's encroachment. He believed that however it may turn out, there would be much pain and suffering.

"Dad, are you okay?" she asked.

"Yes, of course," he said and smiled at her. It's just that I didn't have a very good conversation with Jake on trying to stop that highway."

She sensed that her father was worried about something other than the highway. As she reached out and touched his hand to comfort him, she briefly saw her father's thoughts. Expecting to feel his sadness and worry, she was shocked to see images of terrible destruction, like the conflict she had sensed from the pyramid. She tried to block her senses but was unable to shake the vision.

“But it’ll all work out somehow," Robert said, trying to sound optimistic for his daughter. “Let's head down to the lake. It’s nearly time for Jordan to fly us back."

On the way back, Jordan followed the path of the new highway, and some forty five minutes in, they saw the convoy of trucks heading towards Coppertown. They flew over the town itself, and finally, true to Jake's word, the highway construction team that had already finished nearly five miles of the road to Percipience. Robert looked down intently at the ground.

“Do you see something down there, Dad?” Lauren asked.

“I see a herd of large animals. I think they’re elk. I didn’t realize there were so many down this way. Perhaps we should organize a little hunting trip.”

She didn’t quite understand why her father would have made such a suggestion. There was more than enough big game around Percipience to handle the yearly quotas each hut was given. Still, she didn’t want to disagree and risk upsetting him, especially after his meeting with Jake.

It was dusk when they reached Percipience, and Lauren told her father that she would be late for the evening meal. There was something she needed to do first. She went to the Epoch cabin and knocked on the door. To her surprise, Allison greeted her.

“Hi, Allison. I know it’s getting late, but is Alec around? I need to talk to him. It’s about Epoch, and it’s important."

Allison’s demeanor softened. “I haven’t seen him for the last few hours. He mentioned that he was going over to your greenhouse. If you catch up with him, can you tell him to come and see me before his work shift?”

Allison knew that the friction between Lauren and Alec had all but disappeared since the last trip to the pyramid, and she was unsure what to make of it. She could see that Alec fitted all too well into the Percipience lifestyle and had no intentions of moving back to Epoch. This was something she could never do. The few months spent in Percipience had made her long for home, and the occasional shopping trip that she made to Epoch made her homesickness even worse.

“Okay . . . I’ll let him know," Lauren said and headed to the greenhouse.

When she arrived, Alec was working in the bug farm, “What are you up to in here?” she asked.

Alec’s grin stretched across his face. “The others from the Epoch camp don’t know it, but about a third of their protein for the last month has come from these little crawly creatures. I figured I’ll continue this for another month or so and then break the news to them.”

“You are pure evil," Lauren said with a smile, “but I guess we did do the same thing to you."

“I think it’s the only way to get people to really accept them. If I mentioned it right away, they’d reject the idea, but if I tell them they’ve been eating them for a while, and even commenting on how good they are, their resistance should be much less."

“You’re still evil. By the way, Allison said she needs to see you before you go to work. And can we talk for a minute?”

“Sure," he said, “Let's take a walk."

They started down a path that led into the town center. “Alec, I’m sure you know that nobody from Percipience wants this highway your Dad is building. Do you think there’s any way you could convince him to stop?"

“I doubt it. He’s so focused on it—and it’s not just him. The council and most of Epoch wants it completed too."

“But there must be something you can do. I have a horrible feeling that something awful will happen.” She thought back to the dark feelings that she picked up from her father’s thoughts.

Alec now knew to take what Lauren said seriously. “Awful? Like what?”

“I’m not really sure, but I see a lot of havoc if it’s completed.”

“No one from Epoch would do anything like that. I’m sure that Percipience will be fine,"

“No, not Percipience—the carnage that I see is for Epoch," she said. “I’m getting visions of great loss and sadness. I’m not sure why— maybe some kind of bombing. At least talk to your dad. Maybe get him to slow down the construction to give us a bit of time to figure out what’s going on."

“I honestly can’t see anyone in Percipience doing anything violent.”

Lauren paused for a moment, and then said, “Listen, Alec, I’ve heard people say there’s no way for our two cultures to integrate. And I can see where things could get desperate. There have been some strange activities here lately, like the hunting trip my dad is planning to the South. No one in Percipience has never done anything like that before since there is plenty of large game right around the village.”

“I can try to convince my dad to slow things down, but I can't promise that it’ll do any good," he said. “I’ll talk to him in the next few days and let you know what he says.”

“Thanks.” She stopped and hugged him. “I miss the time we used to spend together." They held each other for a few minutes longer.

“Me too,” he said, remembering the time after the plane accident. He had been happy and content, not only being around Lauren but with life in general. “It seems so long ago, and so much as happened since we first met." He put his hand behind her head and drew her to him and gave her a kiss. Surprised at first, she soon returned his affection with a passion she could no longer hide.

“I’m sorry," he whispered as they drew apart. “I don't know what came over me."

“It’s okay." She tracked her fingers slowly through his hair. “I understand that you’re feeling pulled in several directions. You’re going to have to decide who is right for you, and when you do, let me know." She kissed him again, and they walked in silence back to the village center.

24 - CLANDESTINE OPERATIONS

It was late in the evening when Clyde walked through the park near the town hall. He was on a regular salvage run to see what people had thrown away that he might use or repair. He was almost through the park when he sensed motion near the water tower. Peering into the encroaching darkness, he saw Jake pause at the door to the maintenance room below the tower then go inside.

Thinking it strange, Clyde walked over to the tower. He opened the door, looked in, and noticed movement behind large pipes in the back of the room. He entered quietly and moved between the pipes until he found a dark corner where he could hide while watching Jake take a reading from one of the tanks. This was followed by mutterings before something was dropped into the tank. After a few minutes, Jake turned off the lights and left.

Clyde remained motionless in the darkness in case Jake returned. After a while, he retraced his way towards the door. He turned on the lights and went back to the tank area. He knew nothing about the pipes and tanks, or how anything worked in this room but had a feeling that something was very wrong. He looked into the tank that Jake had paid so much attention to and saw a new tablet on the bottom beside one that was nearly dissolved. He reached in and picked up what remained of the smaller tablet, wrapped it in a rag found on a nearby workbench, and put it into his pocket. Then he retraced his steps, turned off the light, and left the room. He had no idea what the tablet might contain, but he had an idea of who would.

The next morning, Jake rose somewhat later than usual and started the day feeling tired. He had worked hard for the last several weeks and knew that he would need to make some changes. He needed someone trustworthy to share his plans for Epoch and who could take over some of his chores. He immediately ruled out Alec, since he seemed to take a greater interest in Percipience. Jordan, however, was a potential candidate; he had done well in the negotiations for the computer time and in managing the Epoch camp. Jake made a note to himself to have a chat with Jordan the next time he was in Epoch.

When he arrived at his office, he expected to see his desk as he left it the evening before, clean and organized. Nobody else had this expectation, and when he entered the room, he was faced with a growing stack of papers and notes from his secretary on things needing his immediate attention. He sat at his desk and began to flip through the pile. One of the notes was a message informing him that Jordan wanted to talk with him as soon as possible. He couldn't help but smile at the coincidence and hurried to the radio room.

"Jordan, I got your message. What's going on?" he asked.

"Do you have time today to talk about a few things?"

"Sure, how about right now?"

"No, I'd rather do it in person. Alec and I are planning to be there in a few hours anyway." There was a slight hesitation, and then he said, "I'd like to speak with you in private."

Jake was intrigued. "Okay, we'll talk when you get here."

He thought about the conversation on the way back to his desk. While working his way through the morning, he came across an interesting letter from the head of the Re-Discovery Center asking about allocations, especially for the cold fusion project. He laughed to himself and composed a reply saying that he was personally leading the project team. At the last minute, he added that it was not to be worked on by anyone in Re-Discovery since they were already short on resources.

Pleased with himself, he then made a note to release another memo saying that the cold- fusion project could not reproduce the expected result and that they were continuing to work on it. What he didn't divulge was that he had nobody working on the project. He couldn't afford to have "free" power available as this would upset the entire economic basis that Epoch operated on. His disinformation campaign would be carried out for a few more months, and when the highway to Percipience was completed, he would make sure that the machine they had there, apparently working, would be sabotaged.

It was near lunch time when the plane could be heard approaching Epoch. Some people stopped to watch it land and pull up to the dock. It was a common event now, and not as many people paid as much attention as before. Alec, Jordan, and Robert walked up the dock and were greeted by Jake.

"I wasn't expecting to see you, Robert," said Jake with a polished smile.

"I came up for a few days to spend some time in the library at the Re-Discovery Center and to see how the Percipience team is doing. I'll be staying with them." Robert emphasized as he had no intention of having anyone following him while he was in Epoch.

"Very well," Jake said in a permissive tone as he turned to Alec.

"Your mom told me to tell you that she misses you and wants you to spend lunch with her today at the house. I'm sure Koda would like to see you too."

"I'll head up there now," said Alec. Jordan, can you take those papers to Re-Discovery and we can meet here after lunch to load the plane with supplies?"

"I have a couple of memos that I need to go up there too. Stop by my office, Jordan, and I'll give them to you," Jake commented.

Jordan admired how smoothly Jake had handled things. "See you in a few hours," he said to Alec. Then he lifted a box full of papers and started up the dock with Jake towards the town hall.

When they were in his office with the door closed, Jake motioned for him to sit down and then pulled up a chair beside him. "So, what's on your mind?"

"First, I wanted to talk to you in person, since I'm pretty sure that Robert is listening into to our secret radio frequency."

Jake raised his eyebrows. "What makes you think that?"

"A few things—he knows when we're going to make special trips down here. He never seems surprised when I bring up topics that you and I discuss on the radio. And he always has a portable receiver on him. I haven't heard any of the normal Percipience communications on it."

"Not solid proof," Jake said, "but I agree we need to be extra careful about what we're saying."

"Right—and I also wanted to tell you about some things going on up there that seem out of the ordinary."

"Such as?" Jake asked

"They're being very vocal about planning a large hunting trip to the south of Percipience in a few months."

"What's so unusual about that?"

"First off, they're mostly vegetarians. I've spoken with several people from Percipience, and they can't recall there ever being a hunting trip like this before." Jordan said. "I've asked Alec too, and we both think they're using this trip as a cover for something else."

Jake leaned forward and absent-mindedly reorganized items on his desk. "Go on."

"Combine this with whatever was taken from the university in Coppertown, and I'm sure we'd find that they're up to something."

"Hmm . . . well, you did the right thing in coming to talk about this with me. I'll need you to see if you can find out anything more. There must be something somewhere up there that'll help us."

"The people of Percipience don't exactly open up to me," Jordan said. "They're nice enough, but our whole camp is still treated as a bunch of outsiders. I'm monitoring their radio communication and have gone through nearly every building in the village and haven't come up with anything."

"Nearly every building?"

"Well, yes, I've found excuses to visit every clan hut, their greenhouse, the town hall and even their fabrication hub. The only place I haven't been in yet is Robert's lab in the Research Center. It's always locked up if he's not there," Jordan said. "It's one of the few building in Percipience that is locked up. I asked Lauren about it one day, and she said it was locked to keep small kids from the dangerous chemicals inside."

"Yeah, I'll bet," Jake said, "I'm sure that Robert is up to something, and there are probably a few clues in there. See if you can find a way in without attracting too much attention. Take a camera from the Re-Discovery Center with you. It would be great to get some hard evidence."

Jordan nodded his head. "That's a good idea. I'll pick one up along with a few rolls of film. And I'll find some way to get into that lab."

"Excellent!" Jake said, "I'll take precautions here and will let you know if I hear anything. I'm impressed with you, Jordan. When this highway is finished, I'll need a second-in-command to manage everything, and you're my first choice right now."

Jordan smiled at the unexpected compliment.

Jake's thoughts were racing after Jordan left. *I knew that Robert wouldn't give up so easily. It's something I'd do if I were backed into a corner like he is. Epoch may not be the target of an attack either, and if I was him, then there are several sites such as the dam, our power plant, and the coal mine that if disabled, would hurt us.*

Jake drafted several memos, one to the guards at all essential facilities, another to a close friend at Re-Discovery to ask that he watch Robert and find out what he was researching, and one to request that every flight into Epoch be monitored to guarantee that no unusual packages were received. Feeling quite pleased with himself, he tackled his afternoon work.

Alec enjoyed a pleasant lunch with his mother and played with Koda, who had missed him greatly. "Hey, boy, maybe you should move up to Percipience with me." His answer was several wet, sloppy licks to his face. "I think you'd like it up there—lots of kids to play with, and I could introduce you to Lauren."

Things were getting complicated. Though still with Allison, there had been more and more contact with Lauren lately, and he couldn't forget the kiss that night in the woods not long ago. "Maybe you can help me figure this one out," he said to Koda. "But now, I need to get to the radio room and catch up on the logs before heading back out." With one last belly scratch, he said good-bye to Koda and his mother.

As he walked down the hall to the radio room, he passed his father's office. The door was open, and Jake asked him to come in.

"How's it going, Alec? Things have been so busy lately that I haven't had much time to spend with you."

"Pretty well. We could use a couple more people to help with the computer and radio up there. People are starting to wear out from the long shifts."

"I'll see what I can do about that," Jake replied, thinking how well that would fit into his plans.

"The computer is the greatest thing, though—it has so much information, and you can look up things so quickly."

"As soon as that highway is completed, I plan to be one of the first people to drive up there and see everything."

Alec paused before he spoke again. "About that highway, Dad, the people in Percipience aren't in favor of having it finished. Do you think you could slow down the construction so that they'd have more time to get used to the idea?"

Jake was surprised by the comment and thought about how to answer. "Alec, the highway is going to get built. It's vital to both Epoch's and Percipience's growth and survival. But I'm listening to you, so let me see what I can do. I can probably slow it down by a month or two," he said, knowing full well that he would not.

Alec's face brightened at the unexpected response, "Thanks, Dad, I'll see what I can do to about changing their minds."

Jake had hoped for exactly that response. Perhaps Alec will have better luck at convincing some of the people up there that the highway was a good idea.

"But it won't be easy, and I have a feeling that they're planning something bad for Epoch," Alec said.

"Bad? What do you mean?"

"I'm not sure exactly. I was talking to Lauren a while ago, and she told me that she was having visions of great loss here in Epoch. Then there's all the radioactive material that Robert has been gathering. I can't imagine it, but maybe they're thinking of building some kind of dirty bomb."

Alec now had Jake's full attention, and he put this information together with what Jordan had told him earlier. "Do you think they're capable of building it?" he asked.

"Of course they can build it." Alec said, "They managed to get the fusion reactor online within days. Their craftsmanship is better than ours. The real question is whether they're willing to do it. They're a peaceful group of people."

"I see your point. But I've already put out orders for the DC to increase security at our critical interests, and I'll scrutinize the payload on every flight that you and Jordan come in here with. Do your best to convince them that this highway *is* a good thing. And keep your ears open."

Alec agreed to fly back and report any new findings. "And I guess that Jordan already told you that we think Robert is monitoring our radio traffic."

"We talked about it this afternoon."

As Alec was about to leave, he stopped and looked at his father. "Is the highway really the best thing for them, and us, Dad?" He did not wait for an answer before closing the door behind him.

25 - FINAL PUSH

Lauren was worried about her father. Ever since their return from the pyramid with the cold-fusion reactor, he worked around the clock. He was always on his way somewhere, or working on something, whether frequent overnight trips to Epoch, planning for the hunting trip, or his lead-cement work in the Research Center, she had seen very little of him.

When she caught up with him one morning and questioned him, he said that he was trying to get things done before the highway was laid down but promised that all would get back to normal soon. She knew he wasn't telling her the whole truth, but she also knew he would say nothing more.

Lauren was not the only one interested in what Robert was up to, and it took nearly a week for Jordan to figure out a way to get into the Research Center building.

"Ow . . . that hurts!" H watched Lauren as she cleaned the gash on his side in the nursing station.

"She's just trying to help," Kimberly said, holding his hand. "How bad is it?" she asked.

"It looks worse than it is. He's lucky that the stick pierced his side the way it did. Some blood loss, but I think it missed all of his major organs as far as I can tell."

Jordan winced. "You *think* it did?"

Lauren laughed. "You'll be okay. We must watch for infection. You said you tripped on the path and fell?"

"Yeah, just bad luck I guess."

"Well, I've done all I can do with it. You should not be moving around too much for a little while. Why don't you spend the night here? You'll be comfortable on this bed, and I'll check you first thing in the morning."

Jordan would have laughed had it not been for his extensive pain. He had punctured himself with the stick so that he would be treated in the nursing station, which was in the same building as the Research Center. He thought he might have to convince Lauren to let him stay overnight, but luck had provided an invitation.

"I'll be over in the morning too," Kimberly added.

As soon as he was alone, Jordan lay down on the bed and waited at least a half hour before getting up to start his exploration of Robert's lab. It didn't take long before he made his first discovery on one of the laboratory tables. Among a pile of papers, there were crude drawings of what looked like a bomb and mathematical equations besides it. He studied the paper and then explored the rest of the lab. There were other clues, more equations and drawings on the chalk board, and bottles of chemicals that showed the University of Coppertown label, all which confirmed his suspicions that Robert had organized the raid on the university.

Ecstatic over his discoveries, he returned to the nursing station and got the camera out of his pack. He captured several pictures of the laboratory, including the chalk board and chemicals, before lying down for a few hours of sleep.

The next morning, after Lauren examined his wound, he went to the computer hut and found Alec and Allison already there.

"Hey, we didn't expect to see you back here so soon," Alec said.

"Yeah, well, I thought I'd get back here and see if I could talk you into flying me to Epoch this morning. I want to have someone from there look at this wound and give me some proper medicine. That witch doctor Lauren applied some kind of poultice to it, and I don't trust that it will keep an infection out."

"But she knows what she's doing," Alec said. "She managed to take care of me, and I was in pretty rough shape."

The loud slam of the log book interrupted their discussion. Allison let her jealousy get the better of her as she listened to Alec's defense of Lauren.

"I'd still feel better if I could get to Epoch," Jordan said. "You up for some morning flying?"

"Your choice," Alec said. "Allison, can you find someone to take my place here?"

Allison hesitated before replying. "Why don't I find two people, and then I can join you? There are a few things in Epoch that I need to do."

"That would be great," Alec said, knowing that Allison could hardly last a few days without needing something from Epoch.

When Jake heard that Alec and Jordan were arriving in Epoch and that Jordan had been wounded, he made a point to meet with him at the local hospital emergency clinic.

"Bad luck, getting cut like that," he said. "I'm glad you're all right." They were alone in the examining room. "You *did* have an accident, right?"

"Yeah . . . kind of a self-inflicted wound. It was the only way I could think of to get into that lab, and I'm I glad I did it."

"I'm impressed," Jake said. "What did you find?"

"I found a rough sketch of a bomb and a bunch of equations. Also, bottles of chemicals from that university up in Coppertown. I knew they had gotten there before us." He reached into his backpack and handed the camera to Jake. "Here's the hard evidence that you wanted," he said.

"Great! I'll get the pictures developed right away." Jake said.

"What was really interesting was a bunch of equations on the chalk board. It took a while, but I think I know what they're for. They're computations for the right amount of material to make a dirty bomb."

"A dirty bomb?" Jake's voice dropped to a tense whisper. "You mean with nuclear waste or something?"

"Exactly," Jordan said. "Robert has been talking about his lead cement, but that's a cover to get radioactive material. He's going to use that in the bomb. And now he's done the calculations to determine the right amount for an area almost exactly the size of Epoch."

"But how will they get it here? We're checking incoming flights, and I have guard posts up in places on the highway."

"I may have that figured out too," Jordan continued. "I found some old maps of this area in the lab. One of them showed a path outlined that led from Percipience directly to Epoch, but it was placed carefully enough to avoid getting too close to the highway. There were some rough calculations on that too, working out to a little under a month for the journey on foot".

"I guess that's possible," Jake said. "Any idea on timeframe?"

"I'm not sure, but I do know they're planning a big hunting trip in about a month, so that and a month for travel from there to here, maybe two months or so."

"That should be enough time for us to take care of this once and for all," Jake said. "I don't want to escalate this now, though. I'll see if we can get through this peacefully, but if that doesn't work, then we'll be ready."

As Jake was leaving the examining room, he was surprised to find Allison sitting in a chair directly outside.

"Hi," he said. "Are you here to help Jordan back to the plane? I think he'll be ready soon."

"No. Actually, I was wondering if I could have a word with you."

"Sure," Jake said. "Why don't you come with me back to the town office? We can chat along the way."

He started the conversation as they left the hospital. "So what's on your mind?"

"It's Alec. We've both been in Percipience for a while, and he's starting to become much too comfortable up there. Would it be possible for you to assign someone else to take our place, and let us come back to Epoch?"

He was initially surprised by the request, but he knew too that Allison missed being in Epoch. He also suspected a different reason.

"Does this have something to do with Lauren?" he asked.

Allison looked uncomfortable with the question. "Partially, I guess it does," she admitted. "She's been reasonable about Alec and me and has left him pretty much alone, but when they're together, I can see there's something between them. And it's not just about her. Alec is changing so much being up there. He told us the other day that the food he's made for us for the last few months has insects in it!"

"Insects!"

"Yes, and so I'm afraid if he stays up there much longer, I'll never get back here."

"I suspected as much," Jake said, "I must admit you've have been up there quite a while now, and Alec's mom is missing him. I could also use some help here with managing this town, so this may work out well for everyone. Let me find some replacements and I'll let Alec know that you both can leave."

She gave Jake a big hug. "Thank-you! Alec might be a bit upset about this at first, but I'm certain that once we're back here, he'll be his old self again."

Jake felt pleased with the turn of events. He had been wondering how to get Alec out of Percipience, and this was the perfect excuse. He had been concerned about how easily Alec fit in with the Percipience culture, and he didn't want him there if the friction between Epoch and Percipience worsened, which he feared would.

26 - CONNECTED

The ribbon-cutting ceremony for the highway completion at Percipience was much smaller than the ceremony at Epoch when the construction was started. Those that did gather for it consisted of the Epoch team that worked in Percipience, a few elected officials from Epoch, and a few people from Percipience. Jake, Lauren, Alec, Allison, and Kimberly were there if only because they were curious about the circumstances surrounding the event.

The highway ended in a parking lot about a half mile from Percipience's. A crew from Epoch had set up a portable stage for speeches but the elected officials cut the ceremony short when they saw the small attendance, and soon the first of several vehicles pulled in.

Alec and Lauren were surprised to see Clyde emerge from the first truck. He made a gallant, but futile, effort to hold Koda, but the dog had already seen Alec and leapt down and ran to him.

"Hi Clyde!" Lauren said. She smiled and hugged him. "I wasn't expecting to see you here so soon, but I'm glad that you came."

"I really didn't have much choice!" he said. "Epoch's town council, with some prodding from Jake, decided last week that they needed more expansion. They've annexed my property. I could've stayed, but it would have been under their laws, which wouldn't have worked out well."

"Annexed?" Lauren asked.

"Yes, they came in informed me that my property is now theirs. They'd pay me for it, which really doesn't do me any good, and I don't have any say in the matter".

"Sounds horribly unfair," Lauren replied. "What about the others from Percipience who were staying in Clyde Ville?"

“I think they’re going to move back here pretty soon,” he said. “When I left, they were finishing up small art projects they had promised to others. But I’m a refugee now! Do you think there’d be room here for me?”

“Of course! You can stay with my clan for now. I’ll give you the grand tour of Percipience. We can ride on an Air Chair—its running all the time now, thanks to the fusion reactor.

Clyde saw one of the chairs weave its way through the trees on the suspension cable. “So the rumors are true then,” he said. “The official word has been that the reactor up here wasn’t working at all, but I also heard from a few people that it was.”

“It’s been running fine,” Allison said. “Actually, the one that’s powering the Air Chair system isn’t the original but a copy we made from it. There are several more being built right now to power all kinds of things.”

“You’ll just have to show me!” Clyde said. He followed Lauren as she motioned towards town and the promised tour.

As they climbed the stairs to the Air-Chair platform near the town hall, Clyde looked to see if anyone from Epoch was watching them. He reached into his backpack and handed Lauren the tablet he had taken from Epoch’s water tower

“What’s this?” Lauren asked.

“I’m not sure. I was hoping that you’d figure it out.” He told her about his night at the water tower where he witnessed Jake’s activities.

“It’s probably nothing,” she said, “but I’ll get my dad to analyze it and let you know.” She led the way up the stairs to the Air-Chair platform.

****

At the same time, Jake was learning about Percipience with Jordan's guidance.

"I'm amazed at how inefficient things are here," he said. "This village is at least twice the size of Epoch, yet has only a fifth of the population. And if they really need to live in these huts, they could at least have put them closer together."

Jordan shrugged. "They want room between them to grow gardens."

"I haven't seen a church here yet. Do they even have one?"

Robert overheard the question as he came up behind them. "No, we don't."

"Oh, hello, Robert," Jake said. He put on his practiced smile and offered his hand. "We missed you at the ceremony."

Robert ignored the pleasantries. "We don't have a church because we see no need to have a special place to worship. The auditorium serves as the place of worship for several religions up here."

"A fine place you have here, Robert," Jake said, lowering his hand. He continued to smile. "Jordan was going to give me the grand tour. Would you like to come with us?"

"No, I have things to do."

"You must be getting ready for that hunting expedition I've heard about," Jordan said.

"No, we've decided to call that off. I'll try to catch up with you later." He walked briskly away towards the Research Center.

"Interesting," Jake said. "I was certain that hunting trip was their cover for bringing some kind of explosive device into Epoch. I've taken several precautions in light of a possible bomb threat, but I need to know I can count on you if times get tough." Jake said.

"Tough?"

"You and I both know that the people of Percipience don't want us here, and we're going to meet a lot of resistance as expansion moves this way. It might involve our having to bring in security people from the DC, especially now with a real bomb threat, to make sure no one tries to stop us."

"I understand. Of course, you can count on me."

"We'll have to pay Robert a visit before I leave," Jake said. "Now what were we talking about before he showed up?"

"You asked if there was a church here."

"Ah, yes, a church. That will be one of our first orders of business here. We need to bring some proper religion to this group," Jake said. "There's much to do now that the highway is complete. I can imagine daily trips between the two towns, and now that we're connected, I'm expecting there'll be families moving from here to Epoch."

"I'll start scouting a site for the church, and I'll start to make arrangements to make it easy for people to move from here over to Epoch," replied Jordan.

"That's good," Jake said. "Now, let's go and see this so-called cold-fusion reactor."

"It really does work," Jordan said, as they headed towards the reactor hut.

"It may work, but it's something we must keep quiet. I've sent out memos saying that the reactor up here isn't working after all. Free energy will cause nothing but problems for Epoch." Jordan looked at him questioningly.

"Free energy would change the entire way the economy works," Jake said. "If energy was free and decentralized, it would destroy the current infrastructure and the companies that run them."

"I still don't understand," Jordan replied.

"It'll become obvious to you once you have more experience in running a town—perhaps a town like Percipience." Jake gave Jordan a slap on the back and laughed heartily as they entered the reactor's hut.

****

When Allison returned to her cabin after the ribbon-cutting ceremony, she was surprised to see Alec and Koda already there.

"I thought you had to work after the ceremony," she said.

"I was wrong. I guess all the shifts are cancelled today because of the ceremony. But on my way back here, I ran into Robert, and you won't believe what he told me."

"What?"

"I know there's been talk for a while, but it's now official. The elders met last night and decided that Percipience is going to branch off and start up a new village."

"I thought that the whole idea here is to *not* expand," Allison said.

"Well, yes, within a certain area, like this town, but if the new town is far enough away, there'd be little impact, and it would protect their culture in case of some disaster here."

Allison thought back to her earlier conversation with Jake and hoped that he would soon talk to Alec about returning to Epoch.

"It would be a great adventure to be part of that new village," Alec said. "We could take all that we've learned from here *and* Epoch and make it a great place to live."

"We'll just have to see how things go," she replied cautiously.

****

Jake's tour of Percipience had wound its way back to the town center, and he and Jordan stopped at the Research Center.

"Strange," Jordan said. "This door is usually locked."

They entered and saw Richard and a few others working at laboratory benches, but Jordan immediately noticed there were things missing. The board showing bomb drawings had been cleaned and now contained only chemical equations. The boxes labelled from the university in Coppertown and the radioactive sample box were nowhere to be seen.

"Hi, Robert," said Jake. "Jordan gave me the town tour, and it's quite impressive. You've managed to accomplish a great deal with the limited number of people you have."

"We get by," Robert replied. "There are actually some big changes in the works."

"I'm sure," Jake said. "With the road between our two towns now complete, I have no doubt there'll be many changes."

"I wasn't referring to the highway," Robert said. "During a meeting with the elders last night, it was decided to start plans for another village like Percipience."

Both Jake and Jordan were surprised. "Do you think that's a good idea? Especially now with our towns connected," Jordan said.

"There was a long discussion on that topic last night. Yes, this is probably a perfect time."

Jake placed his hand on Jordan's arm. "If that's what you think is best, Robert. You'll have to let me in on all the details when you get them worked out. I need to get back to Epoch, but I'm sure we'll see each other soon." He signaled Jordan to head towards the door.

"Thanks for stopping by," Robert replied without looking up.

When they were outside again, Jordan insisted that many things had changed. "That room has been cleared of all of the things I saw a while ago. And then there's all that talk about a new village."

Jake nodded his head, "I don't know Robert that well, but we've met several times, and something is different about him. He seems much calmer and more defiant."

"What do you think he's up to?" Jordan asked.

"I'm not sure. I wonder if they already have that bomb in Epoch or at some other key target. I'll stop at the DC when I get back this afternoon and will get teams together to do a radiation sweep of the key points. They couldn't have brought a bomb down there without leaving at least a small trace of radiation somewhere. If there *is* a bomb there, we'll find it and then confront him."

27 - SAFEGUARDS

All the problems coming from Epoch, even those that threatened the very existence of the lifestyle in Percipience, could not compare to the frustration that Robert now felt as he sat before the WISE terminal. *What kind of sick person would jumble all of the keys like this*? He slowly pecked in the search term he wanted on the QWERTY keyboard.

Allison listened to another series of groans. "Are you sure you don't want any help over there?"

"No! I'm just fine," he said gruffly. "I need to learn how to use this thing."

The real reason that Robert refused Allison's help was that he was searching for information related to Epoch. A few weeks before, Lauren had given him the tablet brought to her by Clyde and repeated the story of Jake's suspicious behavior in the water tower. Robert had done a series of chemical analyses on the tablet, and its makeup, while organic in nature, did not match anything he had seen before. His trip to the computer hut had been made to see if the WISE system might be helpful.

Perseverance finally paid off as a new article appeared on the screen. It discussed the exact chemical composition that he had found. He read the piece carefully, and by the time he finished, he was more perplexed than when he had started. *Why would someone put this in Epoch's water supply*? It described Oleander, a plant that he had seen on the Re-Discovery campus, which had no known benefits he could see.

He read about some side effects from ingesting the plant, and like a light slowly emerging from a fog, he put the pieces together. "Got you!" he said out loud.

"Pardon?" said Allison.

"Nothing at all." He began to understand the full meaning of what he had found. He quickly returned the terminal to the main screen, put the data disc back on the storage rack, and left the computer hut feeling better than he had in months.

****

Jake was in an excellent mood as he sat at his desk in Epoch. It has been a few weeks since his trip to Percipience, and since then he had immersed himself in expansion plans. The anticipation of economic growth because of a few thousand more consumers of goods would catapult Epoch years beyond what he had originally planned.

The salvage teams were proving to be more productive than he had expected with a regular stream of trucks coming from Coppertown full of recyclable metals and other needed items. Things were moving in a better direction than he could have hoped.

His day was further brightened when he read a memo from the Percipience team stationed in Epoch. They thanked him for letting them visit Epoch, but it was now time for them to return. *Things will finally get back to normal here. Getting Clyde Ville annexed was a brilliant idea if I do say so myself.*

He was brought back to reality by a knock on his office door.

"Come in."

One of the town administrators entered and spoke in a low voice. "You said you wanted to be kept informed about the movement of people between Percipience and us."

"Yes, yes," Jake replied. "What do you have?"

"We have twenty families..." he said before Jake broke in.

"Twenty already? And it's only been a few weeks! That's great news."

"Uh... sir, that's twenty families moving *from* Epoch to Percipience. No one has moved here. Most of the families that moved went up when the Percipience team did."

The man backed away from Jake as his anger exploded. "*What?* Why would anyone want to move to such a backward place?" He slammed his fist on the desk, sending papers flying. "This has to stop right now! I'll get the paperwork approved, but you make sure to get the message out that people who leave Epoch will still be liable for all their debts. That should force them to stay. And if they don't pay, we'll find them and put them in jail!"

"Right away, sir," said the administrator, who realized the perfect moment to leave.

"Moving from Epoch—unbelievable," Jake muttered to himself. Then another thought occurred to him. *Maybe they're working with Percipience on a plan against Epoch. Who knows what kind of crazy ideas they could get into their heads. Who's to say they're not involved in the plan to put a bomb in Epoch and are getting out of town to avoid the blast.*

While thinking it a long shot, he knew it was better to be safe and radioed the DC to send a squad into town with radiation monitors. They were to investigate every inch of the homes of those who had left Epoch. Soldiers from the DC scoured Epoch and the surrounding areas, and so far, they had found nothing.

****

The speed of the migration to Percipience took the elders off guard and they were forced to accelerate their original plans.

Robert and the elders now met daily after dinner. One elder addressed the unexpected number of families relocating to Percipience. "Look, Robert, it was only a few weeks ago when we approved the new town. But we're just not ready to start acting on things yet. We hadn't planned on people coming up here so soon. I think we should consider sending them back for a while."

"No, we're definitely not sending them back." Robert replied. "I know there'll be some short-term pain here, so let's divide them among all our huts and get them immersed into our way of life. We also should get some men down to the new site and start on the construction work."

"The new fusion reactors will help out a lot," another elder added.

"They certainly will," Robert agreed. "We don't have all of the plans made yet, but we can start with basics like getting construction materials ready for the huts and other buildings. And they can start to dig trenches for water lines."

"And we need a team here to start building a barge to bring things down there."

"Exactly," Robert said. "So even without all the plans in place, there's enough work that we know needs to be done."

"But what about materials like copper and pipes?

Robert smiled, "I've worked out that part already. There's is one advantage to that highway. We can now get what we need from Coppertown and get it here easily."

"Won't Jake be upset?" the elder asked.

"He may, but I already have a plan in place that will change his mind."

While the elders were busy working through accelerated plans for the new village, the rest of Percipience was full of excitement and spoke about little else.

Alec told his father as much as he knew when they talked by radio.

"They've found places for the families that moved up here, but I think that most of them will move to the new village as soon as some of the building is completed," he said.

"I still can't believe that people want to go there," Jake replied. "But that's not the reason that I wanted to speak with you."

"What's up?"

"Things are very busy down here with resources coming in from Coppertown, and the highway completed. Since you and Allison have done such a great job up there, I'm filling out the paperwork now to get replacements for you. Both of you can now come back to Epoch and work here."

"Move back to Epoch?" Alec couldn't think of anything else to say. His father had caught him by surprise.

"Yes! I know that your mother will be as very pleased to have you back."

"But Dad, there's so much more that I can do up here," he pleaded.

Jake was adamant. "You and Allison have made enough of a sacrifice for Epoch. It's time to come back home. And I'm going to be glad to have my son back as well. I have a meeting up in the DC in a few minutes. Start packing and try to get back here within the next week."

Alec stared at the radio receiver, realizing that the conversation was over, and there was nothing more that he could say. The last thing he wanted to do was move back to Epoch. What he wanted was to convince Robert to let him and Allison be among the first to move to the new village. *What am I going to do now?*

As he drove to the DC, Jake thought that his conversation with Alec had gone well. The subject of his return to Epoch was now one less thing to worry about. When he reached the command center, there were several captains and lieutenants already gathered around a table that had a map of Epoch and the surrounding area.

"Anything new to report?" he asked.

The second-in-command officer came forward. "We found nothing after searching the homes of people who had already left for Percipience," he said. "It was just like the last two weeks after we went through the whole town."

"It's time to change tactics, then," Jake replied. "We're going to head up to Percipience and take control. We'll have to force Robert to tell us where it is."

There were several nods of agreement from the group. "When?" an officer sked.

"The sooner, the better—probably within a week. We've focused on recruiting and training for several months so we should have the manpower, and I know that we have the firepower. They have barely any weapons there."

28 - CONFRONTATION

Shortly after dawn, trucks arrived at the parking lot near Percipience. Unlike the other vehicles from Epoch that moved construction machines and supplies, these trucks were loaded with soldiers, all dressed in the same forest-green camouflage uniforms and each carrying a gun and several other weapons.

The troop stood at attention after exiting the vehicles. "You all know your assignments and the layout of this village," Jake said. "I want every single leaf turned over until we find that bomb or information on it. Now move out!"

The armed soldiers broke into smaller teams, each with their own assignment, and moved into the forest that spread out towards Percipience.

As Jake headed towards the town center with two armed guards, Alec came running up to them.

"What are you doing?" he asked.

"What are you still doing here? I told you to go back to Epoch. Your mother and I have been expecting you."

"I'm not going back—at least not to live." Alec stated.

"Yes, you are!" Jake's voice was raised. "Now get your things and Allison, and I'll get one of my men to take you back. I don't have time to worry about you right now."

"Allison and I are not going back to Epoch. We're moving to the new village."

Jake laughed humorlessly. "In the first place, it was Allison who asked me to arrange getting both of you back to Epoch."

"What?"

"What do you expect? She wants modern conveniences, stores, clothes, and everything else—and not living like this!"

Alec felt stung by Jake's words. "Neither of you seem to understand anything about Percipience," he said. He left his father as quickly as he could and stormed off in the direction of his cabin.

Jake thought it best to deal with Alec later when he was sure to be feeling less angry. He motioned for the two guards with him, and they continued their way to the town hall. *We're finally going to put an end to all this.* He had begun to gather his small army since first hearing about the bomb threat, and today, Percipience would finally be integrated into Epoch. As he walked along the path, he could hear the men's shouts as they went through the huts and the screams of frightened women and children.

He and his guards arrived at the Research Center and pushed open the door to find Robert at his laboratory bench.

"I was hoping to find you here," Jake said. "Men, start your search!"

Robert jumped to his feet. "What the hell's going on?"

"Did you think you could keep the construction of a bomb a secret? I've known about it for months now, but today your plan comes to an end. I have men searching your whole village, and we'll find it or stay until you tell us where it is."

They heard a gunshot from outside. "Find out what's going on!" Jake yelled to the guards.

Robert watched in astonishment as Jake waved his arms and the men ran outside. Jake pointed at him accusingly and demanded an answer.

"There's no bomb here—at least none that we plan to use on Epoch," Robert said sarcastically.

"Then what are these?" Jake asked. He pulled from his shirt pocket the pictures that Jordan had given him.

Robert glanced at them and smiled broadly. "They're the equations and drawings I scribbled on the board that I saw on the WISE system."

"Why would you do that?"

Just then the guard ran back in and told Jake that a man in Percipience had been shot trying to prevent soldiers from entering his hut.

"Well, that was expected." Jake said, "Get word to the troops to continue, and use force as necessary."

"Enough!" Robert's voice reverberated through the laboratory and everyone fell silent. "You fool! You're so obsessed with profit that you have no idea of what you're doing. It was exactly this kind of narrow-minded thinking that caused everything that led to the Great Loss."

"Now wait a second..." Jake said.

"Shut up! This is over Jake. It's done."

"Glad to hear you're coming around— finally," Jake said

"That's not what I mean, and you know it. You've been so absorbed with Percipience that you've neglected what's happening in your own town." He turned to the guards. "Jake and I need a few minutes—please wait outside."

They looked at Jake, who nodded his approval.

When they had left, he sat down on the nearest workbench. "What are you talking about?"

Robert pulled out a chair from a standing stack and sat down. "Have you seen your latest hospital reports, specifically the data from pre-natal care?"

"What's that got to do with this?" Jake said, waving his arms again.

"They are zero, nobody is showing up. And the reason is that your entire village has been sterilized."

"*Wha-a-at?*"

"You can validate it whenever you want, but I already have, and it's true. All of the women in your town have been sterilized, and in about sixty or seventy years, there will be no one in Epoch."

"I don't believe you!" Jake shouted.

"That's your choice, but you can't change the truth. I designed the drug that was used. It's the same one we use here, so I know it works very reliably. Now, I want you and the rest of your army and construction workers to get out of my town." He could feel his anger building inside him again. "You have until the end of today."

Jake felt dizzy and overwhelmed by what Robert had just told him. All his plans disappeared into nothing within a single moment. Robert could be lying, but to what end? Everything could be found out quickly enough. There would be no point.

"You're a bastard," he finally said. "We're not going down without taking you with us. I'm going to order my guards to kill every male in your village, and then we'll round up the women to use as breeding stock!"

"No, you're not," Robert said. "In fact, what you're going to do is something that you're good at—manipulating people. You will go back to Epoch today and convince the people think that some kind of virus or alien caused the sterility."

"I will not!" Jake bellowed.

"You will, and I'll give you one reason why. Oleander."

Jake sat down quickly but stayed defensive. "What of it, it's just a plant."

"Yes, it's a plant, a pretty one as well. And it's not even native to this area, but it's grown in abundance in your park at the Re-Discovery center. And then, somehow, it ends up in your water supply."

Jake's shoulders slumped.

"It took me a while to figure out the purpose of putting it in the water, and then it dawned on me. With all your tools and technology, Epoch is still strapped for resources, people, and food. Oleander is known to cause heart muscle disease if it's given in the proper dosage. It wouldn't affect your younger population, but it certainly will affect your elderly. So right at the age when people are no longer useful to you, they start having heart problems and die. Very handy for not taking up extra food or staff to take care of them."

Jake knew that if he didn't do as Robert asked, his career and name would be destroyed.

"I have proof from water samples and eye witnesses who've seen you monitor them. You are responsible for putting this poison into the water supply. If you don't do exactly as I say, I'll make sure that everyone in Epoch knows about it."

"I did *not* start this," Jake said. He spat out the words defiantly. "It started decades ago, and I just continued along the path that village managers had already gonc down."

"Just because someone else started it did not mean that you had to continue this monstrous act. You cannot put the blame on someone else." Robert said.

Jake thought for a few minutes and knew he had been beaten at his own game. Revenge was not the answer here. "Okay, we'll be out of here by sundown." He picked himself up and walked out the door.

****

Alec burst through the door of his cabin. "Allison!" he called out loudly.

She ran from their bedroom. "What is it?"

"You asked my father to move us back to Epoch!" He looked at her accusingly.

She felt her mouth go dry and realized her secret had been discovered. "Alec, please listen."

He cut her off before she could say anything more. "You had no right to ask him—especially without even talking to me about it."

"You wouldn't have agreed anyhow," she accused. "Just the other day you were talking about moving to the new village."

"What's wrong with that?"

"I don't want to live this way." Allison waved her hand across the room. "I don't want to eat bugs, and I want my own things. I have nothing here."

Alec stayed silent then walked quickly into the bedroom. He returned a few moments later with his backpack.

"Where are you going?' she demanded. "To Lauren?"

"No." He continued walking towards the door. "I'm not going to her, but I'm leaving here and finally know what I'm going to do. Enjoy your trip back to Epoch."

29 - REVELATION

A month had passed since the confrontation between Robert and Jake, everyone in Percipience had learned of the fertility problem in Epoch. The official word as drafted by Jake was that radiation contamination had created a mutation in a virus, which, in turn, caused the sterilization of all females in the town. They also assured everyone that the devastating consequence was isolated and seemed to have no other effects.

"Why do you think we haven't seen any of this in Percipience?" Lauren asked her father as they sat with Clyde by a fire after the evening meal.

Robert sat back and sighed. "There are things that you need to know that I haven't told you." He looked around to see if anyone might hear their conversation. "The fertility issue in Epoch wasn't a virus or radiation poisoning. It was the same sterility drug we use here."

Clyde sat in stunned silence while Lauren felt a chill slowly creep over her. "Why?"

"Let me explain," said Robert. "About three months ago, the drug was introduced into the water supply in Epoch by the Percipience team living there at the time. I brought them supplies every week, and they'd break into the water tower to mix them into the regular chemicals already in the water."

"Dad! How *could* you? *Why?*" she asked again.

"It was the hardest thing that I've ever done," he replied, "It was not only I but the entire group of elders who agreed that it was our only available course of action. When two different cultures meet, the one more advanced will always dominate the other. This has been true throughout human history—like Europe's expansion into North America. If we want to retain our culture, it's either us or them."

"How about Jake and the report of radiation causing it?" Clyde was finally able to ask though still in shock over the news.

"Jake knows the truth. I've convinced him to leave us alone, and that there's nothing to be gained from revenge."

"What about the bomb? Weren't you planning something?" Lauren asked.

"It was a decoy that we needed for two reasons. Jake isn't stupid—he was expecting us to do something. The bomb was easy to fake and quite believable. The other reason is because of you, Lauren. I'm sorry I had to deceive you, but with your powers, I knew you'd try to warn Epoch about the plan. That's why you didn't see too much of me. Each time we did get together, I concentrated as hard as I could on making a bomb so that you wouldn't find out what was really going on."

Lauren tried to absorb all that her father was saying. She felt as though her breath had been knocked out of her. "You wiped out their entire town," she finally said. "I can't begin to believe, or understand, that you, of all people, could do such a thing."

"There was no other choice, Lauren. We delayed it as long as we could to see if there was any other way." He watched his daughter struggle with his words, and he knew he was unable to comfort her.

Clyde's voice broke into their thoughts. "You need to build some weapons," he said. "You could've used them to protect Percipience against Epoch and avoid having to go down this path. I'm sure there'll be more confrontations. There are other towns out there, you know."

Robert shook his head. "No. Other than a few guns for protection from wildlife, no other mechanized weapons have ever been allowed in Percipience. It's one of the founding principles, just like population control."

"Why is that?" Clyde asked. "How are you supposed to stop others from just walking all over you?"

"If you rely on mechanized weapons for protection from other humans, the situation naturally evolves into an arms race—a terrible waste of lives and resources." Robert felt increasingly uncomfortable with the discussion. His eyes kept watch to see if anyone was approaching, and then his voice dropped to a near-whisper. "You are not to repeat to anyone what I'm about to tell you. This is knowledge that only the elders are supposed to have."

Lauren and Clyde looked at each other and leaned forward simultaneously.

"From what I understand from the books written by our founders," Robert said, "the long-term plan for Percipience's defenses lies with the paranormal powers that you're starting to demonstrate." He pointed at Lauren. "Until we get to that point, the original plan was to be able to threaten intruders with a crippling virus. However, and this's where it gets a bit murky, something happened right around the time of the formation of Percipience, and the virus was released all over the globe. It wasn't just crippling either, it was lethal."

Lauren emitted a sharp yelp, and her father raised his hands to his mouth in a signal to silence her. "The Great Loss!" she said in a strangled whisper. "So it was man made after all, and Richard was to blame for it. He murdered billions of people."

"Yes, it would appear so. I'm guessing that something must have frightened him into wrapping up his plans early. Like not finishing the cold-fusion reactor and setting off the virus worldwide, but we'll never know what that was."

"Wait," Lauren said. "How did we survive the virus attack? I can understand a very small percentage of people in towns like Epoch, but *everyone* in Percipience survived."

"Simple," Robert said, "The antidote has been put in our food since the very beginning, along with a few other chemicals that are supposed to increase our mental and paranormal capacities. It's the reason we have synthetic meat once a week. That is one of the distribution methods of the vaccine."

"At least it makes sense now," Lauren said. "I've wondered why we still had that synthesized meat."

"Hey, what's this about paranormal powers?" Clyde asked. "What can you do?"

"I'm trying to figure that out myself," Lauren said, "I get premonitions regularly now and can influence the way things move a little bit. For instance, I can roll any combination of dice."

He slapped his knees then reached over and clasped Lauren's hands in his. "I've always thought it was possible—I *knew* it! You have to show me tomorrow."

Lauren laughed at Clyde's enthusiasm. "It's a promise."

"These powers are the key to our culture's survival," Robert said, "We also need to expand to make sure that a specific event like an earthquake doesn't wipe out our whole group. That's why the elders decided to start the new village even though we're not quite ready for it. The goal is to have around twenty villages like Percipience throughout North America."

"I'd really like to be part of that new village," Clyde said.

"I'm sure that we can arrange that. There's lots of work to be done, and they can use all the help they can get. I've heard that even Jordan and Kimberly are planning to move there."

Lauren thoughts quickly shifted. "You haven't heard of anyone seeing Alec there, have you?" she asked. "Since the confrontation with Epoch, he seems to have vanished."

Robert looked at her closely. "You miss him, don't you?"

"Very much. There was a deep connection between us, but then he just left without even saying good-bye. I spoke to Allison before she returned to Epoch, and she said they had a big fight and had no idea where he is now."

"I understand he was under a lot of pressure that day," Robert said. "But I do have a bit of a surprise for you."

"What?"

"I know where he is."

"Where?" she said anxiously, "How long have you known? Why didn't you tell me right away?"

Robert laughed "I just found out myself today when some men came back from the new village site. Alec showed up there a few days ago. He must have walked instead of taking the river route. From what I hear, he pretty much took over and is doing a great job. But I would think he could use some help."

Lauren leapt up and threw her arms around her father. "I'm leaving in the morning."

She broke off her hug as she saw a bright light appear on windmill hill and then fade away.

"What was that?" Clyde asked.

"I have no idea," Robert said.

"I have a feeling that someone or something was watching us," Lauren said, "I felt it earlier but did not pay attention to it since I was engrossed in our discussion. Now, though, after that light, the feeling is gone."

An uneasiness crept through all of them as they looked up towards the hill. Each wondering what the light was and what the future would bring.

Appendices

APPENDIX A – AUTHOR'S VIEWPOINT

"Anyone who believes exponential growth can go on forever in a finite world is either a madman or an economist" - Kenneth Boulding, economist.

Though these words are targeted towards economy and the finance community, they could easily be applied to several other key areas of concern in the world today. Our demand for natural resources and food, as well as our impact on the environment, must be fulfilled by the relatively finite capacity of our planet. Harder to quantify, but equally important, is our capacity to adapt to the environmental strains of new technologies, high density populations, and the ever-increasing pace of life.

I believe that the question we must answer is tied to Richard's projection of our state of affairs in 2022. Is it too late? Are we at the point where demands can no longer be met by capacity? If so, what will the impact be? If not, how long do we have until we reach the point of no return? The crucial question is not whether we will have enough fresh water, oil, or corn, or whether we can lead a purpose-filled life, but will it be the same for future generations? Do our current choices and actions make this possible for them?

Our answers will determine how we can prevent surpassing various tipping points, or whether we simply accept that the train has left the station and that we need to focus on preparing for some degree of collapse. These two courses of action, preparation, and prevention, contain similar elements but require different models to be successful.

The answers to these questions are not simple. As mentioned in 2022, there is a large amount of data to process, and it is often conflicting and inconsistent due to different agendas by governments, corporations, scientists, and others. Is it possible to arrive at a clear understanding of global environmental vulnerability, the timeframe left for restoration or collapse, and what further actions we need to undertake? Our ecological sensibilities should at least match, if not surpass, levels of tolerance as consumers.

Human infrastructures based on self-indulgence remain an ominous way of life. When I look around the world today, I'm left with the impression that we don't have an infinite amount of time left to find answers. Several areas seem to be near, or perhaps past, a critical juncture. The question to be answered is *Are we there yet?* You, your children, or your grandchildren could well be burdened by crises involving emergency preparations, or even a collapse.

These concerns led me to write the Percipience book series. In story form, I wanted to see where our current practices would lead, and with the town of Percipience as a plot point, to look at an extreme example of a nature-based culture. Could such a society co-exist with a more consumption and growth-based world?

Together with the environmental and economic differences in Percipience, I have added aspects of fringe science or what some call the paranormal. It remains my opinion that because something cannot be verified through scientific rigor in no way disproves its existence. Interspecies telepathic communications and premonitions are two examples of there being well-documented cases, but both are still scorned by the general scientific community.

A more personal reason for my remaining open-minded is due to an experience that occurred a few years ago. I rarely remember dreams, yet one morning I vividly recalled sitting at a bar and talking to a girl I had never met before. We discussed her having just lost her job and some of the consequential details. Some two weeks after that dream, I went out with friends and after an hour or so, I ran into a girl I didn't know, but who looked familiar. We had almost the same conversation, word for word, that I had dreamed. My ability to finish her sentences on specific subjects shocked her as much as it did me. Do I have "proof" this happened? No. Has it ever happened again? No. But it did happen.

I hope that with time, we will be able to remove the filters in our minds so that they can accept and explore in more detail. Percipience, with its ample leisure time and tight control on human evolution, seemed like a perfect mechanism. The awakening of Lauren's powers is just the beginning.

In the third book of this series, *2232*, there are new challenges for Percipience along with an exploration of some of the current social aspects that are influencing our relationship with this planet and each other. I invite you to explore www.the2222book.com for more information, current updates, and to engage in the discussion.

APPENDIX B – A DIFFERENT APPROACH

It appears, at least to me, that most of the world's population is not too alarmed or overly concerned about the impact we have on this planet. Unlike when there is a terrorist threat or a virus outbreak, I sense that, in general, people do not feel that there is imminent danger that would compel them to take immediate and drastic action.

I believe that one of the reasons for this is that we trust our leaders. Surely if there were problems that would have serious impacts on us in the next few decades they would know about it, inform us and take the appropriate action. Wouldn't they?

- Starting in 2007, the United States and several other countries suffered the worst financial meltdown since 1929. Even with all the regulations and oversight by very smart people, financial instruments were allowed that were directly responsible for the collapse of several major financial institutions and bankruptcy for many individuals.

- There have been extensive studies concluding that a class of pesticides known as neonicotinoids is one of the factors leading to Colony Collapse Disorder in honey bees. The response to this has been varied. In the European Union, the pesticide has been banned yet in the United States there are no current plans to stop its usage.

- In 2013, the NSA PRISM program was exposed showing extensive surveillance activities relating to e-mails and other social media from the general public. Up until this time, there had been numerous denials that such activities happened.

Our leaders are not omnipotent. They do not always foresee problems and they, at times, do not disclose information or take the appropriate action when crises occur. Can we afford to put all our trust in them to guide us to a sustainable path? Perhaps we should not completely rely on them in this critical area and take a more active role ourselves.

To do this, I feel that we need to two things. The first is to evaluate how near we are to a critical juncture in the areas of natural resource usage, pollution, economics or social behavior. The second is to take appropriate action.

It is impossible to evaluate all the data in these areas but there are, however, examples all around us that, in my opinion, tell us that things are not going well and cannot continue much longer. A few of them are listed below.

- The Colorado, Yellow, Teesta and other major rivers have such high irrigation and city water demands that they often no longer flow into the ocean.

- Key natural resources such as copper and phosphorus, which, at current known supplies and usage, have a life of 50-200 years before the planet's supply is effectively exhausted. Related to this, we have now started mining the ocean floor without, in my opinion, understanding the impacts this will have on a fragile eco system.

- The Atlantic Halibut, Bluefin tuna and several species of whales are just a few examples of fish that are on the endangered species list due primarily to over fishing. There are hundreds of reports published in the last few years indicating that the bio-diversity on this planet is decreasing and talk of the next 'Mass Extinction'.

- The "Dead Zone" in the Gulf of Mexico. Caused nearly entirely by agricultural activities along the Mississippi river watershed (roughly 5000 square miles in 2014).

- There is enough mercury in rivers and streams in most populated areas that health organizations publish limits to the number of fish that can be safely eaten from them.

- Small, but one of my personal favorites. If you live in Canada, *until the end of time*, taxpayers will be paying to freeze the ground near Yellowknife to prevent over 200,000 tonnes of arsenic that we have put there from seeping into Northern Canada's waterways. This arsenic is from gold mining operations, and one fifth of one gram is a lethal dose.

- Conservative estimates indicate that by the year 2050 there will be another *billion* people on this planet (United Nations World Population Report). Our current population (January 2015) is 7.3 billion, an extra billion will certainly increase the stress on the planet.

Our leaders try to manage these and other issues through laws, regulations and quotas aimed mostly at corporations using the natural resources to make the things we demand. As individuals, we cannot do this. We can organize rallies and write letters, but I think there are additional and more effective ways. By drastically reducing own consumption and by having open discussions with friends, family and co-workers, I think we can have a dramatic impact.

By drastic reduction, I am referring to a paradigm shift for most of us and a few examples are listed below. Of course, everyone's situation is different so some may not be possible for everyone.

- If you are single, take in a roommate or be one.

- Change your diet to consume far less or no meat.

- Cut your budget for Christmas and birthdays by at least half or more.

- In general, avoid purchasing new and try to find used instead. This goes for cars, houses, electronics, jewelry, clothes and the like.

- If you must buy new, buy the smallest, simplest item you can.

- Move to where you can walk or take public transportation to work.

- Have a discussion with your children regarding your retirement and the possibility of you living with them.

- Pay more attention to the groceries you buy and menu plans to avoid throwing out food that has gone bad.

- Looking for a better rate of return on your investments? Try concentrating on reducing your cost of living instead. It is far easier to reduce the cost of your lifestyle by 25% than to get a 25% increase in rate on return on your investments.

Do you have other suggestions? Please visit www.the2222book.com and remember to engage others in this topic and make them aware of this website.

PERCIPIENCE SERIES CONTINUED - 2232

Time did not dampen his need for revenge. If anything, in the years since the showdown between Epoch and Percipience, his commitment for vengeance was stronger than ever. Like a wolf watching his prey, he patiently waited for the right opportunity to strike back.

With the development of a new defense system for Percipience, Alec and Lauren thought that they would finally be able to concentrate on the challenges within their own village. However, an unexpected telepathic connection and a new riddle change all of that, leading them to the discovery of new technologies and the uncovering of an imminent danger threatening them, their village and the human species.

As the story unfolds, the characters begin to realize the unthinkable. That Richard may have made a fundamental mistake when laying out his plans two hundred years ago. A mistake so significant that it may unravel their very way of life and perhaps may do the same in the real world that we live in now.

Time Lost – Book Four of the Percipience Series

Realizing that they have not gone far enough to save the planet, Richard and the eco-terrorist organization CURE decide to take their fight into the commerce atmosphere, against formidable enemies that are very well prepared.

Independently, the multi-nationals are realizing that environmental issues are starting to put a dent into profits and that there is a real risk to their foundation—growth. They unite to put in place a tried and true solution, war, on a scale that our planet has never seen before.

Just like a game of tug of war, there can only be one winner. But is the rope, in this case the planet, strong enough or is it so frayed that it will be torn apart in this conflict?

Feedback on this book would be appreciated. If you get a moment, please leave a rating and/or review on Amazon, Goodreads or Librarything.

Made in the USA
Charleston, SC
22 December 2016